Also by William Hatchett
Rural Drives: a journey through English housing policy
York Publishing Services, 1998
ISBN 1 902633 57 1   £9.95
Available from Amazon www.amazon.com

William Hatchett

Dragon Rising

Honor Oak

First published in Great Britain by Honor Oak Publishing, 2006.

Cover design by Jez Tucker.

British Library Cataloguing in Publication Data.

A catalogue record for this book is available from the British Library.

ISBN 0 9552297 0 7   978 0 9552297 0 1

Printed and bound by Biddles Ltd, Unit 24, Rollesby Rd, Hardwick Industrial Estate, King's Lyn, Norfolk, PE30 4LS.

To my father

Acknowledgements

Before we begin, I should like to thank Csilla Nagy and Stephanie Hirtopanu for their help with the Hungarian and Romanian elements in this story, respectively; Deirdre Mason for her encouragement and indefatigable proof-reading; Jez Tucker for his technical help and graphic design; Anna for talking to me about publishing; Karina for her patience (!); Caroline for teaching me about dragons; Sonny for his invaluable advice, and, as ever, James.

Oh that my words were now written! oh that they were printed in a book!

Book of Job 19:23

Foreword

Many people thought that my grandfather was mad. I was not one of them. I never met him. But I have spoken to many people who did. They say that he was opinionated but not dogmatic, self-effacing but fond of improabable stories. Born in 1898, he served in the First World War. He fought in the Battle of Loos, survived, and transferred to the Royal Flying Corps, winning a DSO for gallantry. After the war, he worked as a pilot for Imperial Airways. He retired in 1953. He used to say that flying was in his blood, that he was proud to have served his country and that he hated traitors.

I know now why he held these beliefs. One day, in the early 1970s, I was going through his papers in my attic. They had been passed to me by my great uncle, who disliked my grandfather and had never bothered to read them. At the bottom of a trunk, which was stuffed with legal documents, was a thick, somewhat yellowing, typewritten manuscript. I realised, with amazement, that it was a memoir.

A casual reader may say that my grandfather exaggerated and embellished – he certainly did. But his book, which I have finally succeeed in publishing after many years, suggests that he played a part in one of the most curious conspiracies of the twentieth century. My role is not to defend or justify his claims, merely to present them. I am a librarian, so it comes naturally to me. Here, without further ado, is my grandfather's story.

Jonathon Endicott, Ripley, Surrey, 2004

Chapter One

I had few expectations for that night. The weather was wet and I was not feeling particularly happy (it was to do with a failed love affair which I would rather not go into). I had found myself, more or less by accident, at the Royal Geographical Society in Kensington Gore, attending a public lecture. The subject of the lecture interested me. It was an account of an expedition to an outcrop of the Carpathian Mountains in Transylvania. My father, who was an explorer, had visited the region in 1872. Unfortunately, the focus of the talk was bugs. Geoffrey Broadhurst, the entomologist, was an un-prepossessing speaker. He had a round, pale face, a bristling grey moustache and bulging eyes with large pupils (good for seeing in the dark, I conjectured).

I was on the point of slipping quietly away – Broadhurst had been droning through endless projections illustrating small brown insects – when something that he was saying caught my attention. Initially, it was the tone rather than the content of his words. His voice had become raised in pitch. He appeared to be somewhat agitated.

"They were destroying the mountain!" I heard him say. "This was the Devil's Mountain, *Muntele Dracului*. It is viewed with awe by the people of Transylvania! According to their folklore, to disturb the mountain in any way risks bringing a terrifying curse upon one's head."

Broadhurst said that the Devil's Mountain, in the Apuseni range, was one of the world's only known habitats for an extremely rare spider, of the genus something or other. He added, indignantly, that half of the north-western face of the mountain had been removed. It had been converted into a vast open-cast mine.

"From what I could see," Broadhurst said breathlessly, "it is being worked by slave labour. The people whom I saw were

11

shackled and their gang masters carried guns and bull-whips!"

A small gasp passed through the room. Broadhurst was wearing a pale linen jacket that was tight around his shoulders. I saw that he had sweated all the way through it, producing dark patches at the armpits. His face was flushed.

"When I approached the workings an armed guard swore at me, in German, and twisted my arm behind my back. He then smashed my camera with his rifle butt." Broadhurst paused to take a breath. "Of course, I protested both to the British consul in Budapest and to the Hungarian authorities. But do you know what? They denied, categorically, that any mining was taking place. They said that I had either been hallucinating or had made the whole thing up!"

He stared into the half-empty auditorium, appealing for sympathy while realising, perhaps, that he had become a little overwrought.

"I shall not let this matter rest," he said. "It is an outrage that a unique habitat has been desecrated in this way. The leopard spider is one of the only ..."

He was about to lose my interest. I decided to cut loose and take my chances with the rain. I collected my hat and coat and hailed down a cab outside. Broadhurst's lurid story was swirling around in my head as I made my way along Piccadilly to my club in Charles II Street, for a late nightcap.

I don't know if you remember the African and Oriental Exhibition Rooms? Located in Museum Street, they were a minor feature of Bloomsbury, before the First World War. My father had started the business in the 1880s. In the shop premises downstairs he displayed curios from his travels around the world – there were sinister, nail-studded fetishes, war clubs, suits of armour, Samurai swords and, on occasion, shrunken human heads. The London public ogled our exhibits and, not infrequently, bought them. On Tuesday evenings, my father conducted magic lantern lectures in a room upstairs. These occasions are among my earliest memories – gasps as he revealed to his overheated audience scantily dressed tribes women and fearsome pygmies, melting into the shadows of a primordial forest.

One afternoon, it must have a couple of months after the lecture at the Royal Geographical Society, I was sitting in the first-floor office above the sales rooms. I should explain that my father had died the previous autumn, passing his eclectic collection into my somewhat reluctant care. It was just before the evening rush hour. I was vaguely aware of a faint excited hum from the crowds thronging Great Russell Street, the clopping of hooves and the irritating buzz of motors. These sounds, the warmth of the room and my father's idiosyncratic accounts ledger had made me terrifically drowsy. I was actually nodding off to sleep when, suddenly, as if from a dream, a picture swam into my mind.

It was to change my life. I saw, in my mind's eye, a book – a thick, leather-bound volume, with marbled covers. This artefact was extremely familiar to me. It had been part of my imaginative landscape for as long as I could remember. It was the first volume of my father's journals. I do not know, to this day, where the thought came from. But I realised, at that moment, that I must read it. It was on a shelf, only a few feet from where I was sitting. The volume had a black leather spine. My father's name, T.W. Endicott, had been tooled there in gilt letters

The professionally-bound book contained my father's notes on his journey to the Carpathian Mountains and the Black Sea in the 1870s. Its vellum pages were filled to the margins with his spidery, copperplate handwriting. The ink had scarcely faded, although the creamy pages were spotted with damp. When I opened it, a familiar smell wafted to my nostrils – dusty but with an exciting undercurrent, like musk or a rare spice. It was the smell of my father. Whether it was through fate, or an incredible coincidence, I can never know, the book fell open on my desk at precisely the right entry – the 27th of March, 1872.

The page began with some ethnographic notes, comparing Romanians, Magyars, Saxons and Szekelys, the races that shared possession of Transylvania. My father's pen lingered over descriptions of the local women, with their embroidered blouses, long skirts and broad leather belts; he talked of their sparkling white teeth and of their "bewitching" eyes. (Let us be frank, my father was always a ladies' man.)

"Tuesday morning," I read, "Took path to Dumbrava de Sus. Lesser spotted eagles. White storks. Numerous cowslips, primroses and ... (here, a word had been washed away by a droplet of water). Path climbs from churchyard to *Muntele Dracului* or the Devil's Mountain."

The hairs on the nape of my neck stood up. It was the same mountain that Broadhurst had described."Frightening." My father, who was a man of delicate sensibilities, despite his taste for adventure, had underlined the word, twice. "Black summit obscured by heavy cloud. Thunder. Lightning flashes around peak. It is the most desolate ..."

On this page, several words were smudged. Had my father written them sheltering from a raging storm beneath a cliff? Or had he stayed the night in a leaking barn? With difficulty, I made out the following sentences.

"Ascend (?) steep valley. Obtain samples of a dark grey crystal, flecked with red. It is known in Dumbrava de Sus as Blood Stone, or Dragon's Stone. People superstitious. Cross themselves whenever *Muntele Dracului* is mentioned. The mountain is associated with dragons, which are supposed to sleep beneath it!!! They will not touch the stone, or even look at it. Have obtained sample which will polish up ..."

The Blood Stone! I remembered it now. The crystal that my

father had brought back from Transylvania had been one of his favourite objects. He had explained to me, when I was very young, that it was a fragment of hedonite, a rare mineral found in certain remote parts of Eastern Europe. The highly-polished specimen was oval in shape, about three inches in length and an inch wide. The extraordinary thing about it was this. The opaque grey stone had a vermilion core that looked, in a certain light, like a drop of blood. My father told me, solemnly, that the people of Transylvania held that this was dragon's blood. They believed that the stone had magical properties.

This example had been returned from Transylvania in a steamer trunk, with other treasures, via Constantinople. It had been displayed with pieces of rose quartz, jasper, and malachite in one of my father's mineral cabinets. These exhibits were not for sale. The stone's hand-printed label gave no clue to its provenance – it was, as far as the public were concerned, merely a marginally interesting curiosity. The Blood Stone, although I had not lain eyes on it for more than ten years, must still be downstairs, in a seldom-visited corner of the sales room.

I gave up when it was too dark to continue. I must confess, I did not like reading by electric light. It seemed harsh and unnatural to me – an inferior form of daylight. That night, as I drifted off to sleep, I recall seeing a vision of the mist-shrouded peak of the Devil's Mountain. It was intriguing that Broadhurst and my father had been to the same place and that both had had an alarming experience there. In reality, I could do little with the information. However, I did not have to wait long, until the next day in fact, for the next piece of the puzzle to slot into place.

It was mid-afternoon, on a dreary, wet day. The weather had discouraged people from venturing out and trade had been slow. I was sitting in the office doing some paperwork. It must have been about three o'clock when I heard a commotion outside. I distinctly heard a phrase in a foreign language – it seemed to be German, a language I knew a little of from school, although the sentence was composed largely of clicks and hisses. Suddenly, the door burst open. Floyd, my sales assistant, was gripping by the forearm a slightly-built man who was trying to break free.

Floyd, a lad of sixteen from Camden town, was far stronger than his years would have indicated. He was an excellent worker and a model of loyalty. His toothy smile was always a welcome sight. I had come to depend on him. I can remember the scene as clearly as a familiar picture. For I have re-visited it again and again in my mind. Floyd's captive had light-coloured hair and a thin, patrician-looking face. He was wearing buff riding breeches and an olive green jacket, with an upturned collar. On each side of the collar was a curious insignia. It is important later, so I had better describe it. It was a five-pointed or pentacular star, flanked by what looked like dragon's wings.

One would have said, from the man's dress and bearing that he was a cavalry officer, separated from his mount. He was wriggling like an eel and issuing a stream of invectives in broken English.

"This young fool! How dare he!"

He fixed me with a steely grey eye.

"Do you know who I am?"

"My good sir ..." I began.

"I am an assistant to the cultural attaché of his excellence the German Imperial Chancellor, Count Bernhard von Bulow and I ..."

"Please!" I signalled that Floyd should release his quarry.

The patrician brushed his jacket with a manicured hand and puffed out his chest, like a peacock. I saw that there was a faint white scar just above his upper lip.

"He was stealin' sir," said Floyd. "I caught 'im at the back of the shop, near the counter. "

"Pah!" The patrician loaded his exclamation with scorn.

They began to speak at once, competing for my attention, but it was Floyd's voice that broke through.

"... then I seen 'im slipping it into 'is pocket – the Blood Stone."

The Blood Stone! My breath quickened. I felt as if a fist had thumped me in the small of the back.

"Pockets, sir! Ask 'im to empty 'is pockets!"

Floyd moved towards the patrician, whose body stiffened.

"I will not be treated like a criminal," he protested, "by this dirty gutternsipe!"

Floyd looked disgusted and began to protest. I silenced him.

"My *bona fides* are impeccable," said the patrician. "I have a letter in my possession from Count von Bulow himself. And this document specifically ... "

... allows me to pilfer other people's property, I thought. Floyd was regarding me quizzically. What should I do? The patrician had produced a piece of crumpled yellow paper from his breast pocket. He began to unfold it.

"Stop!" I exclaimed. My firmness surprised me. "Your *bona fides* are of no relevance. Either you stole the stone, which is my property, or you did not. It is as simple as that."

The patrician flapped the piece of paper in front of him, like a fan.

"I am sure," he said, sneeringly, "that when Count von Bulow learns of the rude and discourteous manner in which I have been treated ... "

"That is of no interest to me," I said. "May I remind you that we are under the jurisdiction of His Majesty King George V and the Metropolitan Police. The alleged opinions of

'Count' von Bulow are quite irrelevant."

The patrician's eyes were boring into mine.

"Will you be good enough to empty your pockets sir?" I said.

"No!"

I swear that the German's heels clicked together, as if he were on a parade ground.

"Very well then."

My father loved science and inventions. He had been one of the first people in Bloomsbury to have a telephone installed. I now reached towards the mahogany and brass implement.

"Pah!" The patrician's mocking syllable halted the movement of my arm.

"This is absurd!" he said. "It is disgraceful that I, the trusted emissary of the most distinguished ..." I was not listening, neither was Floyd.

As he finished his speech, he sighed heavily and reached into his jacket. Floyd stirred. Revolver, he was thinking. So was I.

However, when the patrician removed his hand he was holding something warm and moist in his fist that was far smaller than a sidearm. He moved forwards a couple of paces and dropped it onto my desk. The smooth stone with its red centre, like an exotic marble, had been a talisman of my youth. Wrapped up with this object were memories of my father's soothing voice, lulling me off to sleep with his tales of adventure. It seemed to regard me, like an eye.

The German was spluttering like a kettle on a hob, his dignity affronted. The distressing affair was resolved in the next few minutes. I did not want to get the police involved. I did not have the patience for their labourious questions and their lugubrious note-taking. Although we both knew that it was a lie, I accepted the German's claim that he had not intended to steal the stone – it had all been an unfortunate mistake. With a cold stare, I told him that he was to leave the premises, immediately. Should he ever return, dire but unspecified consequences would ensue.

The patrician spat out a vile racial epithet as he left my office. Floyd counted with a "dirty Kraut", muttered under his breath. At this time, I am afraid to say, anti-German sentiments were rampaging across London, stirred up by the popular press.

When they had gone, I crossed to the window. I did not turn the light on but stood in the dark, looking out across the street, as my father had done. I had slipped the Blood Stone into my jacket pocket and I now fingered it, like a charm. From now on, I resolved, it would be kept securely locked in the office safe. It had come from one of the earth's strange regions – a place where, according to a reliable authority, men were being worked to death in a slave mine. It must be valuable indeed if the German officer had been willing to risk his liberty to steal it? But what was its true significance?

That evening, I attempted to contact Broadhurst, by telephone, to share with him the discovery that I had made in my father's journal and the story of the attempted theft. I knew that he was a fellow of a Cambridge College. I had obtained, readily enough, the number of the college porter. Although he was about to have his supper, the porter was happy enough to talk to me. But what he told me turned my blood to ice.

"Broadhurst?" he said. "Are you inquiring about his effects?"

"No, what do you mean?'

"He is dead, sir." I was too stunned to reply. "He was found this morning, by my wife." He sniffed. "Hanging from a belt in his rooms, he was. They say he had been there for days. It was the smell that ..."

I shuddered.

"Why? I mean ... how?"

"It looks as though he had taken his own life, sir. He had been agitated of late. Of course, no-one knew him very well. He never had any visitors to speak of, except one Sunday, about a month ago."

"A visitor, you say?"

"Yes, sir." The man paused. He was a patient fellow. He did not seem to mind that I was keeping him from his evening meal.

"It was a foreign gentleman, I think."

"Oh yes." A calamitous feeling was sweeping over me. "Could you describe him for me?"

"Let me see now." He paused. "He was a short chap, with blond hair. He was wearing riding boots. Bloody rude he was. Excuse my language, sir. He swore at me when I asked him what he was doing. He was lurking, you see, on Broadhurst's landing."

"Did he speak German?"

"Yes, I think so. I'm not one for languages myself, sir. I just wish that I had gone into Broadhurst's room to see if he was all right. It seems that this gentleman was the last person to see him alive. I told the police this morning ..."

I let him continue his sentence. He was a troubled soul.

The night after this appalling discovery, I was walking up Charing Cross Road with my friend, Harold Hawkins. We met perhaps once a month, largely to exchange gossip. On this occasion, I had a specific reason to seek his company. I should explain that Harry was the same age as me and that we had met originally at boarding school in Hampshire. He was a journalist on one of London's celebrated newspapers, the *Evening News*. The *News* was owned by Lord Northcliffe. It was a sister paper to the *Daily Mail*.

Harry was a tall, handsome man, with dark hair and a

Mediterranean complexion. His job allowed him to dress fairly casually, but his charming manner made him perfectly at ease, whether he was in the Savoy Hotel or an East End gambling den. Harry's profession required him to be well-versed in subterfuge, which he enjoyed. On one occasion, he had disguised himself as a coal merchant; on another he had hidden in the boughs of an elm tree for twelve hours, staring into a lady's dressing room. "Someone had to do it," he had told me.

He was rarely solvent and always just on the verge of stumbling across "something really big" that would get him onto *The Times*. But it never seemed to happen. I liked Harry's company. He was my touchstone; he always helped me to get to the heart of a complicated question, because that was his job. Sometimes, he was my conscience.

It was a hot, airless evening – almost suffocating. As we walked past the flaring electric lights of the Palace Theatre, I concluded my story. Several things were weighing heavily on my mind – the revelations in the public lecture, the attempted robbery, the death of poor Broadhurst – but I did not know what to do.

For my friend, the situation was abundantly clear. The German officer had attempted to steal my possession. He had almost certain killed Broadhurst, probably because he had unwittingly stumbled across something sinister on his expedition to the Carpathians. Indubitably, said Harry, the next stage in the procedure must be to travel to the Devil's Mountain, to uncover its dark secret. He suggested that the explorer should take a Kodak camera to capture the evidence. Harry sniffed a front page. He would travel there himself, he said, if only ...

He had an inspiration.

"Why don't you go, Austin?"

"What do you mean?"

"To Transylvania. What a jaunt that would be." There was a playful look in his eyes.

"My dear fellow," I said. "Do you seriously think ..." he did not respond. "Do you know where it is? It is hundreds of miles away!"

I explained to Harry that even the Romans had thought of Transylvania as a far-flung place. That's why its name meant "beyond the forest".

Harry shrugged.

"Why, exactly, are you suggesting this?" I said.

"Think about it," said my friend. "Here we have the story of a lifetime and you are scrupling about a week's holiday. Good grief, Austin, what are you, a man or a mouse?"

I declined to answer. I am sure that my friend would not have made the journey himself – as far as I know, he had rarely ventured further from London than Sevenoaks. But his challenge was hard to ignore. And there had always been an element of healthy competition in our relationship.

I stopped.

"Very well, damn you, I will go!"

He greeted the news casually.

"Good man," he said.

"But," I added, "if I get hold of this 'story', as you put, you will not, under any circumstances, take all of the credit. Is that clear?"

I looked into his eyes. I had always been secretly jealous of my friend's occupation. Harry lingered around the Law Courts in the Strand, with barristers and low-lifes; he wrote about Dreadnoughts steaming through Scapa Flow. He witnessed "unspeakable acts" that took place in the opium dens of Limehouse, although moral scruples did not normally allow him to describe them.

Harry tipped back the brim of his hat. "My dear Austin," he said, "I can assure you that you that you will be the hero of the hour. By the time I have finished with you, you will be a cross between Lord Kitchener and Florence Nightingale. You will be plastered across every newspaper from here to ..." he paused. He loved to exaggerate. "From here to Harare."

We both laughed. It was mad. But I would do it. I am a stubborn person, with a strong sense of right and wrong, and once I have made a decision, I usually stick to it. Also, as Harry had said, it would be "fun" – except that we were now in the middle of a swelteringly hot summer and that the armed powers of Europe were gearing themselves up for the largest war that the world had ever seen.

I would leave the Exhibition Rooms in the hands of Floyd. We agreed that I would send telegrams back to Harry on my travels. I should be back in two weeks.

"That's settled then," Harry said.

"Oh yes, quite."

"Good. I say ..." A sheepish grin spread across his features. "I was down at Epsom on Saturday and that last race ..."

I was already putting my hand in my jacket pocket.

"How much?"

"Five bob should do the trick."

I sighed.

"That's the ticket." Harry took the two half-crowns and placed them in his pocket.

"Would you like a drink, up at my club?"

I nodded.

"Come on then."

Harry set off at brisk clip, down Old Compton Street. His club was a dive compared to mine. It was a place where actors and chorus girls mingled with theatrical agents and impresarios. I followed him, as always.

Chapter Two

I decided to make a will before I left: "I, Austin J. Endicott, being of sound mind (!), do hereby bequeath, etcetera ..." It seemed like a sensible thing to do. It was also a good way of taking stock of what I had achieved during my twenty-six years on the planet.

On one level, my life had been uneventful – born in London, boarding school, Oxford University. My father had had me very late and I had grown up somewhat in his shadow. He had often shown disappointment that I had never attempted to imitate his exploits – his journey to Japan in the 1880s, for example, where he was received by Emperor Mitsuhito. Perhaps, on reflection, the Transylvanian adventure, was a way of making up for the lack of incident and exoticism in my life. It had been a source of regret to my father that my older brother, Godfrey, was even more averse to risk than I was. Godfrey had discovered his vocation as a solicitor. I found him a sour man. We had never been close.

In 1912, when he was dying from a tropical fever, my father had called both of us up to his room. Godfrey remained at the foot of the bed. I moved forwards, at my father's request, and allowed him to clutch my hand. My father's white face was covered in beads of sweat; his eyeballs were as yellow as Coleman's mustard. In a hoarse voice, he explained that he was leaving the Exhibition Rooms to me, the younger brother. Godfrey's face was a picture of bitterness. He swept from the room and left the house, without saying a word.

Godfrey was married to a joyless Welsh woman from Calvinist stock. They had a daughter, called Mary. Despite the sternness of her parents, she was a delightful creature. I absolutely adored her. That is why I named her, in the will, as the sole beneficiary of my worldly goods. Some people may find it strange that I, an allegedly rational person, left to a seven-year-old girl a flourishing West End business, a villa in Highbury and a motor car. Perhaps it was a way, unconsciously, of inflicting further pain upon Godfrey, who had always vexed me with his moods and silences.

Having settled my affairs – Floyd was delighted to be left in charge of the Exhibition Rooms – I left England on the 29th of July, 1914. It was an extraordinary time. The Austrians had been baiting the Serbians for weeks and the Russian army was about to mobilise. Once Germany became involved, our fleet would clash with theirs in the North Sea and then ...

My heart was pounding as I waited for a motor taxi to take me, two leather suitcases and a bulging knapsack, down to London Bridge Station. It was just after dawn; the beginning of a bright, warm day. We drove in silence down the Kingsland Road, where Roman legions had once trod. At the station, newspaper vendors were laying out their wares. I glanced at the rumours of war with a feeling of foreboding. I took the train to Dover, a steam packet to Calais, and a further train to St. Lazare station in Paris. St. Lazare had the same excited buzz as London Bridge. There was an unnatural vitality in the air, faintly tinged with hysteria.

When I awoke the next morning, in a swaying sleeper car, I was in Germany. It was a bad time to be travelling in these parts. Officials viewed me with extreme suspicion. I had never been abroad before. I viewed the fields rolling along next to the train with interested incomprehension, like a man scanning one of Mr Whistler's *Nocturnes*. Germany passed by quickly. I was fascinated to watch the white-rimmed Alps steal up on the train. In Austria, my mood lightened. The women's blouses were as crisp and gleaming as the snow and the sky was cobalt.

It had taken my father several weeks to make the same journey – his journal spoke of disreputable inns and rumours of highwaymen. In no time, I was tracking the Danube across an endless plain, as flat as a table top, and crossing into Hungary. It was in Budapest's busy eastern railway station that one of my suitcases was "lost" (I could not resolve the problem with my limited German in the short time available). This, in retrospect, was a signal that life was becoming less predictable, as I progressed eastwards.

The train to Nagyvarad, which was the last major town before Transylvania, was infuriatingly slow. Cars and lorries seemed to be unheard of in this primitive region, which had yet to see the age of steam. Peasants in their round hats stared at the train as if it were a diabolical invention. The harvest was beginning. Beneath cloudless skies, the burgeoning fields were being reaped by hand, as they had been for thousands of years.

I entered the border town of Nagyvarad exactly five days after leaving my house in Highbury. It was the 3d of August. Nagyvarad seemed interesting, although I did not linger there for very long. It had a medieval flavour, with a taste of the Austrian baroque in its towered and turreted buildings. This was the end of the line, as far as the train was concerned. I made a forlorn figure, standing with my remaining suitcase and knapsack in the imposing entrance to the station.

It was mid afternoon and fiendishly hot. Sweat was puddling in my arm-pits, moistening the interior of my felt hat and trickling down my forehead. I paused here for an hour or so, wondering what to do next. I sensed, intuitively, that the disreputable characters who lingered around the station would rob me as soon as spit and that the extravagantly uniformed railway officials, with their moustaches and peaked caps, were all on the make.

I had been confidently informed by Harry that my knowledge of Latin and French would make it relatively easy for me to be understood in this part of the world. Harry was talking rot! This region had once been part of Romania. It had subsequently been invaded by Hungary. Its inhabitants therefore spoke a mixture of Romanian and Hungarian – two entirely unrelated languages. Whatever these people spoke, French was useless as a *lingua franca*. It could just as easily have been ancient Greek. And German was not getting me very far either. I could see what they were at – the sly farmers, the beggars and the station tarts in their straw bonnets – but I could not talk to them. I was beginning to doubt the wisdom of the whole enterprise.

A man approached me. He was wearing an arresting combination of clothes – a cowboy hat, a short jacket, baggy black trousers and riding boots. I was about to dismiss him as I already had numerous peddlers of strange foodstuffs and alleged lucky charms. That, however, would have been a mistake. The man had a luxuriant curving moustache and eyes of the deepest brown, almost black. He was a gypsy. Happily for me, he had picked up a little English on his travels. After a brief exchange, he led me across the street, to what looked like a farm cart, pulled by a venerable grey horse.

In a trice, the animal was pulling us down a broad avenue, towards the town square. The gypsy asked me whether Mr Campbell-Bannerman was the Prime Minister of Great Britain (he was not). He smiled, evidently proud of Nagyvarad, which, he said, was famed for its artists and writers and had earned the sobriquet "little Paris". We crossed a broad stone bridge, traversing the Sebes Koros river.

That night, I stayed in the town's most opulent hotel – the Black Vulture. Directly opposite the town hall, the building made a dramatic statement with its yellow walls, metal balustrades and curved windows, set into scalloped recesses. It was vast. Inside, were marble staircases, plush red carpets and velvet curtains; it was like a miniature palace. I had a reasonable dinner, accompanied by a local tokay, whose sweetness became tolerable after the third glass. After a long bath, I enjoyed a good night's sleep, in a bed that was pleasingly motionless. In the morning, I opened the shutters and studied the yellow and white stonework of a fine building across the river. It was bright, pristine world. I felt happy,

Later, I made my way along the willow-fringed river to the dilapidated inn from which the coach to Kolozsvar, in the interior of Transylvania, would depart. My fellow travellers were an elderly woman of stern expression, accompanying her shy young niece or grand daughter, and a black-robed priest with a prolific grey beard that almost reached his navel. It seems incredible that a journey of less than a hundred miles took four days! At first, we followed the Sebes Koros river through a landscape of hay meadows and rustic hamlets. The land around us was flat, but one was keenly aware of a rim of purple mountains stealing up from the horizon.

Often, when the coach stopped, we would be offered fruit or home-made cheese, held up to the window by a pair of brown forearms. The priest would mutter and look away. The old lady, who smelled of mothballs, would follow his example. She would cross herself to ward off evil if a stranger so much as looked at her for too long; her poor young charge was held in check by constant slaps and reproaches.

On the first night, we stopped at a place that was little more than a barn. After this, we entered a region of oak and beech woods. At times, the forest became so dense that it almost blocked out the daylight. Kolozsvar sits at the edge of the great Transylvanian plateau. It is said to have been founded by the Romans. I did not see much of it, for it was dark when we arrived. It was a relief to be liberated from the oppressive and airless coach. I must say, the fact that I was regarded by the priest and his disciple as an embodiment of evil had begun to prey upon me.

The next stage of the journey was a delight. It was a trip in a hired pony and trap to the mountain village of Dumbrava de Sus. My driver was cheerful. What a relief! And he knew a few words of German. The road was steep. Pine forests clung to the shoulders of fertile valleys. In fresh bright meadows, I was able to identify flowers that had been recorded in my father's journal. There were fields of gentians and ox-eye daisies, misted with butterflies; higher up were saxifrage, wild orchids, alpine buttercups and edelweiss.

Dumbrava de Sus means "the upper wood" and it is an appropriate name. The village sits on a triangular plateau high in the Apuseni mountains, lapped at its edges by seas of birch trees. One can often detect the hand of the Saxons in its houses, with their steeply-pitched roofs and tiled walls. Its Orthodox church looks curious to English eyes, for it is made of wood, with a pointed spire resembling a squat pyramid. The dark form of the Devil's Mountain seems to lour over the village, dominating it like a gloomy stranger.

I bid my new friend farewell and stood, with my suitcase and knapsack at the end of the village's main street. I had already decided to seek accommodation at an inn known as the Pine, if it was still here, where my father had stayed fifty years before. His journal said that it was at the upper end of the village high street, close to the church. From my father's description, it had not changed at all. It was a solid building with rubble walls and a crude, hand-painted sign. The eves of the inn were low enough to brush against one's head. One entered an antique world which had been barely touched by the present century, or even the previous one. I liked the inn at once and could see why my father would have done so.

My room was squeezed under the roof and had a sloping ceiling. There was a note of piety – a dark wooden crucifix on the whitewashed wall. Through the small window, I could make out the triangular peak of the Devil's Mountain, marbled with snow, like a miniature Matterhorn. The view brought a lump to my throat. Tomorrow, I must go there and take a snapshot of the hedonite quarry, if it existed. I wondered whether my father had felt a chill of apprehension at the same cloud-wreathed vision.

I was ravenous after the journey. After a quick wash and brush up (fortunately, I had not lost my soap and shaving kit in Budapest) I went downstairs and sat, expectantly, at a massive beech table. Incredibly, the girl who had taken my order seemed to know a little English. I would say that she was about seventeen years old. She blushed as we exchanged greetings. She was very shy. I indicated to her, by rubbing my stomach, that I was hungry.

She smiled, radiantly, realising what I wanted. That is when I first noticed her eyes. They were as blue as glacier ice, beneath curly, light brown hair, which spilled onto her shoulders. Her figure was trim but voluptuous, flattered by a clinging apron. She was certainly a beauty. A few minutes later, a bowl arrived. It contained a tepid substance, the colour of window putty. The unappetising mush had been garnished with crusty strips of bacon fat. I knew from my guidebook that this must be mamaliga, a native Romanian dish made from crushed cornmeal. It tasted foul. I grinned through clenched teeth as I ate it. Would I like some more? Of course! I ate a second helping, merely because I wished to please the inn girl. We glanced at each other shyly, as I chewed on the perverted porridge. It tasted like a cow's udder.

"Ileana!" A stern voice came from the back of the inn. From the tone of her voice, I guessed it must be the girl's mother. She darted away, with a final lingering glance. My heart surged. It would painful to be parted from her, even for a few minutes.

I set out early the following morning, before the sun had fully risen. Following directions in my father's journal, I made my way to the Orthodox church. My goal was the north-western face of the Devil's Mountain. I had been thinking about little else for weeks. With a tingle of anticipation, I pushed through a carved wooden lych-gate and walked through the church-yard. I was already sweating – I was wearing a Norfolk jacket, a flannel shirt and thick moleskin trousers, in preparation for high altitudes.

The path skirted the side of a valley, rising through scented firs and spruces. I had read that the brown bears in these mountains could kill a man, but there would be little I could do should I encounter one. I had no weapon in my knapsack, only a rain-proof cape, some dried fruit, a canteen and a "map" that I had obtained, with great difficulty, in London. Following Harry's advice, I had also brought a collapsible Kodak camera. For reading purposes, I carried one of my favourite books, Ovid's *Metamorphoses*. The map was virtually useless, but, in any case, I did not need it. My goal loomed inescapably ahead. Trespassing upon the flanks of the mountain, I felt as small and vulnerable as an insect.

After a few minutes, the path broke out of the trees and into the open. A stupendous and unexpected vista now appeared, as if a huge map of Transylvania had been unfolded in front of me. I stood and gaped, as the sun breasted the mountains to the east, casting vast purple shadows of the distant peaks. The shadows flexed like a giant's fingers across an immense plain, which was a sparkling patchwork of brown, green and silver. My spirits lifted then. For I saw my place in a larger picture; I saw how the ancients could characterise the sun, the sky and the mountains as gods.

As I climbed higher, the weather seemed to deteriorate. Perhaps it was always drear and chill here, like the blasted heath at the beginning of Macbeth. The path became harder to follow, winding its way through scree slopes and shattered boulders. At this altitude, only stunted juniper and bilberry could survive, but, ultimately, even that meagre vegetation petered out and I entered a lonely world streaked with snow.

Having been several times to the English Lake District, I knew my limits as a rock climber. And I was now close to them. Soon, the track disappeared entirely. I was ascending an ever-steepening gradient, towards a notch or col at the head of the valley. The nails on my boot soles slid on the limestone rocks; my hands became numb and bruised as I jammed them into cracks to pull myself up.

As the rocks darkened, the going became harder and harder. I realised that the peak was not going to give up its secret without a long and perilous struggle. And indeed, the final way to the col was blocked by a formidable crag, as grim and sheer as a factory wall. I was dispirited and almost gave up. But I remember imagining my father's hand on my shoulder and seeing him frown at me, in my mind's eye. Was I really going to let him down?

What was I going to do? I sighed and lifted my head, to study the lie of the land, standing on a slanting doorstep of rock, with a horrifying drop below. It took a few moments. Then I noticed something. Just to my right, a narrow gully dissected the cliff. The fissure, which was beaded with icicles and dripping with freezing water, was little more than a foot wide. Perhaps it would be possible to jam my arm or shoulder into this and to make my way slowly up the crag?

Very well, I thought. I squeezed my shoulder into the crack. I gritted my teeth and squirmed and wriggled like fury. Within seconds I was drenched to the skin and my teeth were chattering like a magpie. But it appeared to be working. There was a way up! There usually is. Sometimes my hands found a secure hold and sometimes my feet. But rarely both. It was a long hard, slog – easily the most dangerous climb of my life. But it seemed that divine intervention had placed hand and foot holds in just the right places. My strength was about to expire as I approached the top of the crack. It was a close run thing, as my father used to say. But, at last, I reached the summit. With a sigh of relief, I hauled myself up and threw myself onto a delightfully flat surface, where I lay gasping for breath

It must have been at least a minute before I opened my eyes. Lying on the rock, I had become aware of something odd. It was a low-pitched vibration that seemed to come from the heart of the mountain, as if it were alive. When I stood up, I saw the reason.

Ahead of me was a vast, open-cast mine, just as Broadhurst had described. It was an astonishing, almost Biblical scene. I saw hundreds, if not thousands, of men. Some were scaling wooden ladders, with baskets slung over their shoulders; some were prising at the mountain with picks or mattocks; others were lowering full baskets on ropes.

I could hear the harsh commands of gang leaders; I could see sweat glinting on their bare, dirt-blackened skin. Far below were hoppers and the metal roofs of processing sheds. A railway line which terminated here disappeared into a broad, u-shaped valley, leading to the west. Broadhurst had not exaggerated. The entire flank of the mountain was thickly covered with ladders, platforms and men. They were not free men, I felt sure of that from their groans and cries, but slaves, like the Egyptian fellahin who had built the pyramids, in the service of a ruthless civilisation.

It was a little after midday by my pocket watch. I was a long way here from the sunlit meadows and smooth-trunked birches of Dumbrava de Sus. Clouds clung to the snow-capped peak of the mountain. In this infernal region, one could barely see where the mountain ended and the sky began. It was time to take a photograph. Although in this poor light, it would hardly be a very good one. I knew one thing – that I never wished to return here. Was it my imagination, or had it started to rain? I felt a cold, wet drop on my cheek. Then I felt another sensation. A sharp crack on the back of my head. It is my last memory from that day. I fell forwards, stumbling into a great black void, as it rushed up to meet me.

Chapter Three

There was an appalling pain in my skull. My first instinct was to touch the wound that was certainly there. However, there was an impediment – my hands had been tied together at the back of a chair, which, in turn, was attached to the floor.

Was it evening or morning? It was hard to tell. I was in a wooden structure – a hut or a cabin. To my right, was a square, dusty window. If I craned my stiff, aching neck, I could make out a small patch of mountain and sky. I could also hear an eerie murmuring sound. It took me a long time to discern what it was. It was not the wind, but the sound of the slave workers, scraping the Devil's Mountain into their wicker baskets. If one listened closely, one could distinguish individual voices and even, I fancied, the flick of whips, followed by gasps of pain. I had time, in the hours that followed, to speculate upon this work. Why, for example, was the mining operation not using explosives to prise the hedonite loose?

The grey light from the little window diminished; the sound outside rose to a peak and then died away, as the workers were corralled back to their sleeping quarters. Soon, it was quite dark and there were no more human sounds, only zephyrs caressing the mountains and the distant baying of wolves. Now, without the chink of window for company, the desperate nature of my situation struck home to me, and the discomfort – a searing in my wrists, which were tightly bound with cord, and a throbbing in my head and limbs. I knew that as the hours progressed the temperature would drop. I was not prepared for a night high in the mountains. Freezing cold would add to my discomfort.

After a very long time, I heard a bolt being drawn back. Two men entered the hut, illuminated by the glow of a spirit lamp. One was tall and fair-haired; the other dark. Beneath their greatcoats, they wore greenish grey tunics with buttoned down collars. Both had peaked mountain caps. I could see from the marks on his shoulders that the taller man was a sergeant. He took the shorter man's carbine and directed him to place a metal canteen on the table and to untie me. The officer spoke a gutteral form of German. I was not pleased to hear that language again. The food they had brought was scarcely edible – it was a watery soup, containing pieces of gristle. But it was bliss to be untied, however briefly.

After I had eaten, I rubbed the deep red indentations on my wrists and stretched my stiff legs. I tried a few questions. What regiment were the soldiers from? Why was I being held? The men must have been ordered not to talk to me. They responded merely by looking nervously away. Soon, the shorter man tied me up again. Then they left. A heavy feeling of gloom now engulfed me. Those who were pillaging the Devil's Mountain had murdered poor Broadhurst. How could I escape the same fate? It would probably be at dawn, with a single bullet to the head. In the icy darkness, I did not know whether to sleep, or to seek to extend my last conscious hours upon the planet. I think that I entered a kind of trance, rather like that which had overtaken me on the road to Kolozsvar.

Just before dawn, I felt my shoulders being roughly shaken and someone's warm breath on my ear. In the half-light, I made out a man, like a wraith. He was unshaven and wore a brown leather coat. Terror gripped me. Was this it? Was I to die? The man placed a finger to his lips and pointed to the door. I realised that I was being rescued. He freed me with a few quick strokes of a clasp knife and put a finger to his lips. The intruder picked up the rifle that he had placed against the table and bade me follow him outside.

A ghastly site greeted us – a man's upturned white face, staring up from a spreading pool of blood. I guessed at once that the guard's throat had been slit from ear to ear by my rescuer. Although my limbs were stiff and unyielding, I

36

followed his nimble form. No-one was about. We passed a row of wooden barracks and made our way down a track. My rescuer pointed to a heap of large boulders at the base of a steep slope. I gathered that we must climb over them. My muscles were ill-equipped for such a task. However, I knew that in a few more minutes the camp would be awake. I seemed to hear my father's soft voice urging me on and, I swear, I felt him lift me, bodily, by the armpits, over the top of the nearest rock. After half an hour or so, we stopped. Pain has erased the precise details of the journey from my mind, but I recall feeling hugely relieved at the prospect of rest. We passed through a small opening and entered a large, cool chamber in the rocks.

I don't know if you have ever slept in a cave, or lived in one? The Apuseni mountains are scattered with them, for it is limestone country, where rivers disappear without trace into sink holes and pass for miles underground. The interior of this cavern was about the size of a small church hall. And it was surprisingly comfortable.

That first morning, at my rescuer's invitation, I flung myself down on a bed of ferns covered with animal skins. I must have slept for almost twelve hours, because when I woke up, it was evening. A delicious smell greeted my nostrils – that of rabbit stew bubbling in a cauldron. As I stretched my limbs, a friendly voice beckoned me to the cave's entrance.

I was soon to learn that four people lived here – Vasile, Peter, Radu and Florin. All came from the village of Dumbrava de Sus. Vasile was the leader of the little band. He was a blacksmith in his normal life. He was a brawny man with a shock of black hair over his ruddy face. Radu was the brother of Ileana, the girl at the inn. Florin was only twelve, but, to all intents and purposes, he was regarded as a man.

Moving from the sleeping chamber, I saw that a fire had

been made close to the cave's entrance. Four firearms were resting against the wall. They looked like ancient Martini-Henrys – breech-loading rifles, formerly used by the British army. The men were eating silently. Shadows from the fire danced across their faces. Soon, I was welcomed like a long lost brother into their group and a steaming bowl was thrust into my hands.

"English ..." I did not know if it was a statement or a question. The speaker was Vasile, who was looking me up and down. His hair was like thatch.

"Yes," I said. "I am from London." I felt foolish, like some fop who lives off his father's estates.

"It is good, yes ..." Vasile was pointing at my stew.

"It is very good ... thank you."

I could see the way ahead. These generous people would offer me things and make simple statements. I would indicate my pleasure. They would express their approval.

"Have you ever been to Baker Street?"

"I beg your pardon?"

I was astonished. The question had come from a serious-looking young man, with unkempt brown hair. He was wearing rimless spectacles. Twin bandoliers criss-crossed his dark green battle tunic.

"Baker Street. The home of Mr Sherlock Holmes."

"It is close to my office," I said. "But you must know that there is no such place as 221B, where Holmes is supposed to live. It is a made-up address."

"Of course I know that." The young man looked pained. He stretched out a hand for me to shake.

"I am Radu," he said.

Patiently, and in perfect English, Radu introduced me to the others. He explained to me that it had been Peter, the man in the leather coat, who had saved me from the Germans. When I had arrived in the village, the news had spread rapidly from house to house. On the day I had climbed the Devil's Mountain, Peter had followed me. He had observed me scale the cliff – of course, there was an easier and quicker way to the col – and had watched as I was cracked on the head by a German soldier. He had then hidden, biding his time until the right moment to rescue me.

As we ate the delicious stew, Radu told me that he was studying medicine at the University of Bucharest and that he was extremely fond of the stories of Sir Arthur Conan Doyle. He had come up from the village a week before to join the other men. Their intention, he said, was to disrupt the mining activity on the Devil's Mountain. He explained that the soldiers who had captured me were the pride of the German army – members of Wurttemberg Mountain Battalion.

The soldiers had been stationed here since 1912. Military engineers had begun the open-cast mine, to remove hedonite from the mountain. They had constructed a special railway, which, ultimately, connected the mine to Germany. The railway's route, running to the west of the peak, was known by local people as the *Valea de Fier*, or the Valley of Iron. From 1913, slave labourers, mainly Slavs from Serbia, had been put to work from dawn to dusk, harvesting the mountain's grey mineral. Those who were too ill or exhausted to continue were cast aside to die.

"But why?" I asked "do the Germans want the hedonite so much that they are prepared to violate the laws of human decency to get it?"

Vasile stirred. He tried to join the conversation but his English was not up to it. Radu explained what he was attempting to tell me.

"We believe that this hedonite is a magic rock ... we call it the stone of the devil. We believe that it belongs to dragons and is coloured by their blood. Our legends say that if the stone is removed from the mountain, the dragons will rise up from the ground and ..."

"But that does not account for why the Germans want the stuff so much," I said. "And surely you do not believe this ..."

"Of course not," said Radu. "I am a scientist." He leaned forwards. "I believe that there is energy locked into the mineral. I think that the Germans must be making some kind of armament, a special bomb. That is why they are taking the hedonite back to Germany. But to achieve their task, they must mine a large quantity of the material. I think that the explosive element in the mineral is ..."

Vasile coughed. Whether this was because Radu was being indiscreet or because he thought the theory was untrue, I was not sure.

"It is sleep time," said Vasile. "Our English friend must rest. Florin ..." He switched to his native Romanian.

Carrying a candle, the smiling boy led me to the back of the cave and to my comfortable bed. He was a cheerful soul. I tried to talk to him. I even told him the name of my favourite football team, Tottenham Hotspur, and mimed kicking a ball, knowing what boys like. He must have thought that I was mad. Lying in absolute darkness, I wondered when, or if, I would see the girl at the inn again. I drifted off to sleep with the scent of the bubbling rabbit stew, woodsmoke and dampness in my nostrils and a comforting image of her face floating through my mind. I felt safe and slept as soundly as I had ever done.

The next morning, which, by my journal, was the 10th of August, I awoke early. My body was still smarting all over but I felt strangely cheerful. Radu was awake too. I followed him outside. Radu and I had breakfast together – bread and soft white cheese. We were perched on a large, flat rock, over-looking the Valley of Iron. The peak of the Devil's Mountain cast a long shadow here. But as the sun rose this retreated and the valley became progressively illuminated, as if by a sweeping searchlight. It was pleasant to sit on the rock, as the sun warmed us. I felt at ease with Radu, as if I had known him for a long time.

Running along the valley, was the railway that the Germans had constructed. Next to the railway was a road. I could see that it had been churned to dust by German lorries and carts. The road was yellow. Bathed by the morning sun, the mountains turned to emerald green, patterned by grey crags and dark patches of forest. A tiny black speck was wheeling in the heavens. Radu told me that it was an eagle – the lord of the mountains. I breathed deeply, clearing the London cobwebs from my lungs. What a strange fate it had been to bring me, in a few days, from the world's largest and most crowded city to these remote and beautiful mountains. My hands were still trembling. The fear of imminent death had changed something inside me, perhaps permanently. At least I was safe now, I told myself.

"Radu?" I said, "your sister, Ileana, does she, I mean is she...?"

"You mean, is she married?" Radu skimmed a small stone into the void beneath us. "No. Although she has many admirers, I think."

"She is very beautiful," I said, hesitantly.

"She is a stunner." Radu smiled. "I know that she is fond of you, Mr Endicott."

"Really? How?"

"Because Peter told me. Apparently, she cannot stop talking about you."

"Where did she learn English?"

"I have taught her some words. She is fascinated by English things. We both are."

"Why is that?"

Radu shrugged. He then explained that he, his sister and

41

their mother had moved to their mountain home from the town of Cluj Napoca, known to the Magyars, or Hungarians, as Kolozsvar. They had only lived in Dumbrava de Sus for five years. The inn had formerly belonged to Radu's grandfather. He explained that people in the village did not take readily to outsiders.

"The same is true in English villages, I think," I said, "although I do not really know. I am a Londoner."

"I should love to go to London, Mr Endicott."

"I should like to show you Baker Street," I said. "But I am afraid you would be very disappointed. There is nothing much to see there."

It seemed strange thinking about London in such a beautiful, wide-open place. The young Romanian loved to practice English phrases. He must have been saving them up. He pointed above to his right, to an overhanging promontory of rock.

"You see there?" he said.

"Yes."

"We call that rock the camel. Do you see, it is above the railhead, where the Germans load hedonite onto the trains? There is a small cave beneath it. We have placed a ton of dynamite there, Mr Endicott. We are going to blow it up, soon. The avalanche will destroy the railhead and the processing sheds." Radu was scowling. "That will stop the Germans from stealing our mountain."

"I see."

I was about to say something, when I heard a curious noise. I looked down. It was a motorbike, strangely enough, buzzing its way along the road like a small brown bug. Soon, more vehicles appeared – a second motorbike and two heavy lorries. After them, came a wagon drawn by four horses. I was shocked to see that it was towing a large mountain gun, or howitzer. There was a mule train next, carrying ammunition and baggage. Mounted officers in German uniforms clustered around it. They were sweeping the sides of the valley with their field glasses. We must conceal ourselves immediately. We would be lucky if the battery had not spotted us.

"Radu!"

I had noticed something else. A track climbed from the road. It passed directly beneath the rock upon which we were sitting. A boy was running up it for his life. It was Florin! I was horrified to hear a popping noise, as a machine gun, which was mounted on one of the lorries, opened fire. We watched as a stream of heavy-calibre bullets splattered along the track, getting closer and closer to the boy. Florin's arms pumped, as tufts of white dust followed his progress. Bullets ricocheted around his feet. By a miracle, none hit him. Finally, he reached us, gasping for breath. We heaved him to safety.

"Back to the cave?"

Radu nodded. To return there, we must run along a narrow track. The first part of the route was somewhat exposed. But fortunately the machine gun was at the extreme limit of its range. Radu went first, clutching Florin's hand. I followed them. The machine-gunner fired off a few optimistic bursts but soon gave up. In a few seconds, we were safe. It was not heard to guess what had happened. The Dumbravans' hiding place must have been discovered and a detachment of Wurttembergers sent to finish them off. They would pulverise the cave's entrance with their howitzer and train their machine gun upon anyone who tried to escape.

The cool air in the cave touched my skin like balm. I had not run like that for years. My lungs were burning and my heart felt as if it would burst. There was now an urgent conversation between Vasile and Radu. It was not hard to guess what was being said. It was clear that we must flee for our lives. In a matter of seconds, Vasile, Radu, Peter and Florin had gathered up their possessions, including the antique rifles. Escape would be perilous. As soon as we were in the open, the Germans would be able to see us.

Radu took my arm. To my surprise, he did not lead me in the direction of fresh air but the other way, towards the back of the cave. Vasile led the group. He was holding up a lantern with one of his thick brown arms. Close to where I had slept was a small fissure, behind a boulder. I had not noticed it before. We squeezed through the gap, one by one and entered a narrow passage.

Chapter Four

Had it not been for the lantern, we would have been as blind as moles. It was still hard for me to see anything, since I was at the rear of the group. The walls were wet to the touch. Generally, it was possible to stand upright, but sometimes we had to twist our way around obstructions. I do not suffer from claustrophobia. But it was disconcerting to think that we were the human equivalents of earthworms, with millions of tons of rocks above our heads. We had been walking for a long time, perhaps half an hour, when the quality of the air changed. It was cooler and fresher and we became aware of a gentle murmur of flowing water.

The roof of the passage was higher here, the floor smoother. I was not expecting what came next. Without warning, we had entered an astonishing chamber. In my recollection, it was the same dimensions as the interior of a cathedral and equally awe-inspiring. The roof of the chamber was a dazzling white. It reflected back the light from Vasile's lantern, magnifying it a thousand-fold. The roof was actually formed from thousands of stalactites, varying in size from tree trunk width to tiny, fragile filaments. Stalagmites rose up to meet them. One recognised natural forms in the calcified rock. The columns were patterned with striations and bulges, each as unique as a snowdrop or a flower.

"It is beautiful, yes?" Radu's words interrupted my reverie.

"We call this place the bear's grotto."

"Why?"

Vasile moved his lamp to illuminate a recess to our left. I gasped. Its flickering light revealed a mound of bones. Even with my limited knowledge, I could discern the skulls and rib-cages of a collection of large animals. The poor creatures must have become trapped here and died of starvation.

"Don't worry, Mr Endicott." Radu read my thoughts. "You

are quite safe. The bones are hundreds of years old. Do you like this place?"

I was lost for words. The interior of St Paul's cathedral is one of London's most impressive sights. In my opinion, the bear's grotto, with its glistening, soaring roof matched Wren's great cupola in scale and majesty.

"Come." Radu tugged at my sleeve.

There was something else that I should describe. It was the source of the noise we had heard earlier – a broad but shallow stream. Its water, which was extraordinarily clear, flowed away from us and disappeared into an inky void at the far side of the grotto. Vasile said something in Romanian. I now saw, close to where we were standing, a boat – a long wooden skiff. It must have been brought here by the Dumbravans for just such an eventuality – a rapid escape. The four of us lifted and dragged the heavy vessel towards the water. We released it with a satisfying splash. Radu grinned. His teeth, I should have noted earlier, were crooked and discoloured, like an Englishman's.

"It is like the Thames, Mr Endicott, yes?"

I looked down. Gold and silver pebbles sparkled like gemstones through the clear water. In truth, it was more like a trout stream running through chalk than London's mighty river.

"Have you ever read *Three Men in a Boat*?"

"Of course," I said. "But there are five of us."

Vasile, who had been holding the boat with a painter, handed down the rifles one by one and some other personal effects. He then clambered aboard. He was a large man. His weight took the boat's gunwale almost to the water's surface. He pushed us off and Radu and I began to paddle. It was an easy task, for we were running with the current. All that was required was a modicum of steering. The stream ran through the centre of the grotto, rather like the nave of a church. Where the chancel would be, the roof came down dramatically to meet us. We now entered a cleft. The current flowed faster, as if we were being sucked into a drain. I was somewhat alarmed. Radu assured me that we were perfectly safe. He had made this journey many times before. The roof was white and smooth. At times, we could almost touch it; at other times, the passage had the dimensions of a railway tunnel.

An hour or so must have passed in this manner – I must say, it was a pleasant journey. There was something hypnotic about the rippling murmur of the water and the passage of the bone-white roof above our heads. Vasile sat in the prow, holding up the lantern, in front of Peter. His broad arm never seemed to tire. Florin sat behind behind Radu and I, trailing his fingers in the water. I now know why Vasile was so attentive. He was watching for the exact point at which we must stop.

Suddenly, he made a gesture with his hand. Radu twisted his paddle, so that it acted as a brake. I followed suit. We bumped against the cave wall and came to a halt. An iron ring had been set into the rock here. Vasile grasped it and tied up the boat, as Radu and I held our paddles against the current. What now, I wondered? Radu pointed upwards. I received a shock. Above us was a huge, wedge-shaped chimney. It must be hundreds of feet high. A flimsy-looking wooden ladder began just above the ring, attached to the wall. I could not see the extent of it. It simply vanished into utter blackness, at the limit of one's vision.

"Surely we are not ..."

"Yes, we are. Look, it is easy."

Florin scrambled past us. Without the slightest hesitation he began to scale the ladder. He looked down, with a cheeky grin.

"Go on, Mr Endicott. I will follow you."

Radu gave my arm an encouraging squeeze. I stood up and took a deep breath. I don't know whether you have ever scaled the exterior of an industrial chimney? That was the magnitude of the task ahead of me, except that I would not be standing on firm iron staples but on rungs like flimsy chestnut pales, bound to the ladder's uprights with twine. When Vasile mounted the ladder, weighed down by three rifles, it creaked appallingly. There was a moment's silence. Then he laughed.

It does not do to exercise the imagination too much when one is climbing. I tried to dismiss obvious questions, such as how the home-made ladder had been fixed to the rock. The only thing to do was to grit one's teeth, limit the purview of one's vision and move up mechanically, rung by rung. Vasile had fixed the lantern to his leather belt. It swung rhythmically, its yellow light dancing on the walls.

It was fortunate that I could not see too far above, or below. I think that clear illumination would have made the task impossible. Its scale was too huge. I felt like an ant ascending a table leg. At one point, reaching blindly for a rung above my head, it seemed that I could not go on. It was not a conscious decision. It was simply a physical manifestation of terror. My legs were trembling uncontrollably; I was engulfed by nausea.

"Don't give up, Mr Endicott, we are nearly there."

I was certain that Radu was lying. What was awaiting us? Grass? Fresh air? It was only such visions that allowed me to continue. The final rung of the ladder came as a surprise. My fingers reached up to discover – rock! Fear now vanished. The ladder terminated with a flat ledge. I had no desire to see where I had come from, merely to pull myself up and wriggle forwards, until I was convinced that I was safe.

We were all out of breath, except for Florin. I felt sick. Vasile grasped me around the shoulders, like the captain of a cricket team congratulating one of his batsmen. We were not in daylight, or anywhere close to it. We were in a broad, square passage-way which had apparently been carved through the mountain with chisels. Metal braziers were attached to the walls. The floor was as smooth and flat as if it had been made from flagstones. I had the impression that we were in a medieval castle. The other thing I should say is that it was uncomfortably warm. I turned to see that Radu's face, like mine, was covered with perspiration.

"Why is it so hot?" I said.

His expression was inscrutable. "You will soon find out, Mr Endicott. Please continue."

With each step, it grew hotter. Soon, the temperature was almost unbearable. It became difficult to see what lay ahead because I had to shield my face with my hand. We heard a sound like the roar of a blast furnace. Perhaps it was a blast furnace. At the end of the passage was a curious yellow glow, the colour of saffron. Were we in hell? The thought did cross my mind. Young Florin reached our goal first, seemingly unconcerned by the heat. We stopped behind him. My clothes were dripping wet, the skin on my face was smarting, as if I had been staring into a bonfire.

I shall never forget the sight that confronted us. We were standing, effectively, on a narrow ledge. It protruded over the edge of the largest chasm I have ever seen in my life – a hole the size of an inverted mountain. If you have ever looked down from whispering gallery in St Paul's cathedral, you will have an idea of what I saw, except that the scale should be magnified by at least three.

An inconceivable distance below us was a sea of orange lava. It boiled and spat, like the surface of the sun. There was a strong, almost over-powering smell of sulphur. One could not, in fact, look down for very long. It was too painful for one's eyes. Even the backs of my hands were uncomfortably hot. I looked up. I had been blinded by the liquid fire and everything was now tinged with green. It was impossible to see a roof, because it was so far away, although there must be one.

"We are now at the heart of the Devil's Mountain, Mr Endicott," Radu explained to me. He had to shout in my ear, through cupped hands. "It is hollow you see."

A colossal noise issued from the fiery depths – an eruption of lava. It sounded like the largest tree in the world, falling to earth with a splintering crash.

"It is hot, yes?"

Vasile seemed happy. As a blacksmith, he was in his element. His face was scarlet. His blue eyes were sparkling.

"We must walk across." He pointed ahead.

"I'm sorry?"

I have omitted, again, to mention a salient detail. There was a bridge! It may be hard to believe, but a race of hardy lunatics had found a way of traversing the fiery abyss. It was a rope bridge, made, essentially, from the same materials that had been used to fashion the ladder – slats of wood and twine. Close to, one saw its limitations. The bridge, which was furnished with two rope handrails, was no more than three feet wide. The thing was swaying before any of us even set foot on it. Its middle section was obscured by a heat haze; the opposite end was barely visible. To say that this edifice was not up to its alloted task is an under-statement. It was like a dreadnought made from jelly. I like Romanians. But if they are famed for anything, it is not engineering.

"I am not going over that," I started to say. "There is no way ..."

Radu addressed me as soberly as a family solicitor.

"I am afraid that, in the circumstances, there is no alternative, Mr Endicott."

He had a point, when one considered the options. To return would mean descending a mine-shaft on a ladder made from matchsticks, making an exhausting river journey against a strong tide and, finally, facing a large calibre machine gun, trained on the entrance of a cave.

"Look!"

I turned around. Florin had already set off. He was scurrying across the bridge, like a rabbit flushed from a cornfield. Florin never looked back. The bridge bucked like a horse under the impact of his footfalls. He was soon the size of a toy soldier. But, as the three of us watched, something dreadful happened – an event that one would not have predicted. Florin had almost reached the halfway point of his journey when we heard the appalling sound of wood splintering. One or more of the bridge's thin planks must have given way!

Florin's body dropped through. He reached out to save himself. For a moment, the boy was suspended by one arm from the handrail. I shall never forget the sight of his tiny black legs waving. Before I had breathed out, he had lost his grip and fallen. The eerie thing was, there was no scream. At first his body, a spread-eagled silhouette, appeared to float. The descent seemed to take an age. He diminished to a dot against a livid orange background. Then he was gone. The ultimate impact could not be seen, or heard. One could only imagine it.

It was Vasile who screamed. He had loved the boy like his own son. The blacksmith released a sound that I should never like to hear again. It was an animal expression of utter despair. The noise echoed around our heads. We did not, however, have time to gather our thoughts. For, as we watched, a flaming shape arranged itself from the ocean of magma, a thousand feet below. I know that this will seem scarcely credible. It was a weird creature – a dragon of flame. Perhaps the ancients' salamander is the closest approximation to what we saw, or the griffin, which is seen in heraldry. The vermilion animal ascended gracefully. It climbed in a spiral, with steady beats of its scaly wings. It took its time. We saw it from all angles. By the time it had reached our level, we were aware of its scale – it was the size of two London omnibuses.

The dragon was made from fire, except for its fathomless obsidian eyes. It looked straight at us and blinked, once. We stared into the creature's soul and it looked into ours. With a mighty, heart-stopping roar, it breathed out a column of flame, the length of a football pitch. This was not to harm us, I now believe – but to show that it could. The dragon left us. It wafted, like a crimson leaf, into the upper reaches of the vast vault above our heads and vanished. At once, a low rumble began, almost below the frequency that the human ear can discern. The whole mountain was gently quaking, like the engine room of a great ship. Soon, a hailstorm of rocks began to clatter around us, onto the ledge.

"Mr Endicott!" It was the first time I had seen fear in Radu's eyes. "I think it is time for us to go."

"Across there?"

"Yes! It is the only way out."

Vasile led the way. He had composed himself now. It was clear that the bridge would not stay in one piece for very long. Vasile tested a plank with his boot and set off, methodically. We stayed together. That way, at least we would be united in death. There are no gradations of horror. It is merely present or not. I would say that walking across that flimsy, swaying pathway over a flaming abyss ranks with the most frightening episodes of my life.

The mountain was vibrating like a set of giant pistons. Two missing planks indicated where Florin had met his end. We picked our way across this gap, without comment. At its centre, the bridge swayed like a hammock. In the final hundred yards, as I pulled my way up a steep gradient, I was certain that we would die. The mountain would blow its top. We would be flung from the bridge, like sycamore seeds, and burnt to a cinder.

I have never been so relieved to touch the earth. Vasile

lifted me by the shoulders and set me down on solid ground. A passage, mirroring the one on the other side of the bridge, lay ahead of us. Its floor was littered with boulders shaken from the roof. We ran, hearing the first of a series of thunderous explosions, as if the mountain were clearing its chest.

Chapter Five

When I woke up, I was greeted by a wonderful sight. Ileana, the girl from the inn, was leaning over me. My first visual impressions were of her blue eyes and tumbling auburn hair. Above her head was a sloping ceiling, behind it was a simple wooden crucifix. I realised that I was in the attic room of the Pine, although I had no recollection of having gone to bed. Morning light slanted across the rough ceiling from the tiny window. There was a faint smell of woodsmoke and blossom. It was a pleasant way to wake up. I looked into her unblinking eyes.

"Good morning," I murmured.

"Good ..." She echoed the first word, then faltered. We both laughed.

"It is a nice day,' I said. It was a banal phrase. But accurate. "The sun is very hot."

"Yes, it is."

I could scarcely believe it. We were having a conversation! The idea of breakfast must have come into our minds at the same time. Ileana did not know the word for it. But I knew that she would learn very quickly. I knew, too, that I would like to learn her language – it couldn't be that difficult. She asked me if I was hungry – *iti este foame*, in Romanian. A little, I indicated. It was not true. I was ravenous. However, I would rather have gone on looking into her eyes than eaten the world's most sumptuous banquet. She touched my brow with the back of her hand to see if I had a fever. She frowned as she concentrated on this task, her face close to mine.

My other memory from that morning is one of pain. I was covered with scratches and bruises and there were red welts on my wrists from where I had been tied up. My body was afflicted by a miscellany of aches and pains; I felt as if a large animal had rolled over me in the night. I was also desperately tired. I meant to get up after Ileana had left the room – a bird was cooing outside the window, and I wished to investigate the source of the sound. But I made the mistake of lying back on my pillow. Within seconds, I was fast asleep.

Recent experiences – the ascent of the mountain, my imprisonment, the journey through the caves, the crimson dragon – must have been working down through the deepest layers of my mind, melding with memories, sub-conscious images and instincts. I do not remember dreaming. My sleep was too deep for that. I do remember waking up and panicking, not knowing where I was.

My body jerked, trying to free itself from imaginary bonds. My mind had told me that I was tied up and that I was about to die, from a German bullet. My body contracted. I heard myself cry out. Gingerly, I opened my eyes. It was dark in the room and oppressively airless and hot. Ileana must have closed the shutters, to facilitate my rest. When I saw the crucifix, I realised where I was. I felt safe then and drifted back to sleep.

When I next woke up, there were two people in the room. Ileana was wearing a starched, snow-white dress. She had tied her hair back. I saw how fresh and unblemished her skin was. It almost seemed to glow. Radu, her brother, was wearing a dark, sober suit. He was standing close to the bed,

"Good morning, Mr Endicott."

Morning? I must have slept for 24 hours! The sounds and rhythms of the Pine reassured me. Within its thick stone walls, I always enjoyed the deepest rest of my life.

"It is Sunday," Radu explained. "Ileana and I are going to church. But I wished to see you first. How are you?"

"I am extremely well," I said. "A little bruised perhaps."

Ileana edged forwards. In her hands was a blue and white ceramic bowl, covered with a white cloth. Smiling, she withdrew the cloth to reveal the bowl's contents – four of the ripest, most succulent plums I had ever seen. Their skin was purple, shading to black.

"It is your breakfast." Ileana giggled. "It is good?"

"It is very good!" I wanted to hug her.

There was a moment of awkwardness.

"As I said, Mr Endicott," Radu announced, "we are going to church. Before we leave, I would like to thank you for the part you played in our escape."

"No, thank you." I said. "Really, it was nothing. It is you who have helped me."

"Not at all." He looked at me gravely. "You have rendered us a great service."

"I do have certain contacts in London," I replied. "I shall try to communicate to the outside world what has been happening here. But apart from that ..."

The problem was, I reflected, who would believe me? German soldiers were one thing. But dragons emerging from fiery lakes? I did not really believe what we had seen myself.

"Anything that you can do in that regard, Mr Endicott, would be very much appreciated."

Radu's diction was peculiar. It had been learned partly from detective stories and also from books on English etiquette and letter writing. He smiled, knowing that he had come up with an apposite phrase.

"The slave mine," I said. "Have you informed the authorities about it?"

"Mr Endicott," he said, "there is something that you must understand – officials in Budapest are fully aware of what is going on here. But they choose to keep it secret. Do you think that they care about us here, in this remote province of Austro-Hungary?"

A fierce look crossed his face. It denoted hatred for the Hungarian oppressors of the formerly Romanian territory of Transylvania.

"Then perhaps it is in Bucharest that we should tell this story," I said.

He contemplated my suggestion. Bucharest, the capital of Romania, must have seemed impossibly remote from Dumbrava de Sus to most of the villagers. It was hundreds of miles away – the other side of the formidable mountain ranges that cradle Transylvania like a horseshoe.

A thought came to him. "But there is something I must tell you. Some good news."

"Oh yes, what is that?" I said.

What Radu now told me strained my credulity to the limit. He said that while we had been inside the Devil's Mountain, a vent had opened up in the side of the peak. Through this chasm had flowed a river of molten rock. The lava had swept everything from its path – the loading bays and warehouses, the railhead beneath the quarry and, ultimately, the barracks of the Wurrtemberg Battalion. Hundreds of German soldiers had been obliterated.

This geological event had not affected the slave mine, which was higher up the mountain. Seeing that most of their captors had been killed, the slave workers had broken loose. They were now making their way to freedom. Some half-starved creatures had already clambered their way to Dumbrava de Sus.

It was Florin's death, Radu said, that had made these events happen. In ancient times, villagers had made sacrificial offerings to the dragons that lived in the Devil's Mountain. There had been a small chapel deep in its interior and a priestly caste had resided there. He was vague on the details, which were shrouded in legend. However, it was easy to imagine bearded men in hooded cloaks, the chanting of congregations echoing through the chapel; a roughly-hewn stone alter. Florin's fall from the rope bridge, explained Radu, must have been viewed as a sacrifice by the dragons. In response, they had unleashed a stream of lava upon the soldiers who were violating their sacred ground.

The people of the village, he explained, never removed hedonite from the mountain. To do so was thought to make the dragons angry. I thought of the specimen of hedonite that was locked in my safe in London – the Blood Stone. Was it destined to bring bad luck to those who possessed it? I resolved that, one day, I would carry the stone back to Dumbrava de Sus. I would toss it into the flaming cauldron at the heart of the mountain.

I would be able to see for myself, Radu said, the destruction that the volcanic eruption had wrought. Magma was creeping along the Valley of Iron; the peak of the mountain was wreathed in smoke. I could verify this by peering through the window. There was indeed a thick haze around the mountain's summit. It was the only blemish on an azure sky, like a smudged thumb-print.

Radu looked at his watch.

"Mr Endicott," he said, "I am sorry but ..."

"I know. You must not be late."

Radu and Ileana made a handsome couple in their best Sunday clothes. I noticed, that morning, similarities between the two. There was a formality in their manner. But they both spoke rapidly and were quick to laugh.

A bell began to toll.

"Mr Endicott," said Radu. "Would you like to meet us after church?"

"Of course," I said.

"Capital!"

"We shall see you in an hour then."

"Yes, splendid."

He shook my hand. For a moment, Ileana glanced back at me from the doorway. She smiled shyly. Putting on my clothes, I was surprised to discover that that the trousers and jacket I had worn the day before had been washed and pressed. When I unfolded my trousers, something drifted down from them to the floor – it was a tiny, blue pressed flower. I realised why Ileana had smiled at me. I had no wallet – it had been stolen by the Germans – so I wrapped the flower in a piece of folded paper. I placed it in my shirt pocket, next to my heart.

We took the same path that I had used four days before. Behind the church, the path forked into two. One branch climbed steeply towards the Devil's Mountain, the other twisted through a birch forest, a place of cool green shade. This route soon took one to a mountain stream. The stream was perfectly clear. It passed beneath crumbling limestone cliffs and lapped against broad banks of water-smoothed pebbles. Ileana told me that villagers had swum and washed their clothes here for generations. They had always used the path for their Sunday walks and secret assignations.

At a particularly beautiful spot, a crude bridge crossed the stream. Thinking of the swaying rope contraption inside the Devil's Mountain made me shudder. We sat close to the bridge, on a grassy bank covered with yellow flowers. They looked to me like leopard's bane. We had held hands on our walk. It had started when I had helped her to negotiate a rough part of the track. Now, I took one of her hands again.

There was something ineffably graceful in the way that Ileana walked, in how she would gently touch a flower with her fingertips and carry its scent to her face and in how she would dab cool water from the stream onto her skin. I was convinced that she was a dryad or nereid. But I did not tell her this. Once magic is ensnared in words, it is usually lost.

Using simple language, I tried to describe my house in London and my occupation. I said that it had to do with collecting old things. I must have sounded like a rag and bone ban. She already knew that London was inconceivable huge –

the largest city in the world. She seemed to have a vague awareness of some its well-known landmarks. Perhaps Radu had conveyed his knowledge of the city to her, from the pages of Conan Doyle. She would have gained, from him, an impression of swirling fogs, of wood-paneled interiors and of sinister, cobbled alley-ways. How could I describe my London to her and my favourite pursuits – bathing in the pond on Hampstead Heath; motor trips to the countryside; the view at dawn from Primrose Hill, when the sleeping giant roused itself, in a shimmering mist, for another day of bustle and banter?

"Would you like to go there," I said, "after, I mean when ..."

I could see, from her enthusiastic response, that she understood.

"Yes, Mr ..."

"Please, call me Austin. I know it will be hard for you to travel from here and to leave your mother. But I do not mean just for a visit, I mean ..."

Did she understand what I was trying to say? That I never wanted to be parted from her blue eyes and her sweet smile?

"I would like to go, yes ..."

"Thank you!"

I squeezed her fingers. I had never felt such joy. A surge of it passed through my body. It threatened to lift me up, so that I could look down, like an eagle, on the mountain, the woods, the little village and the pointed spire of its simple church, peeping through the trees.

Chapter Six

The next few days were among the happiest of my life. I spent most of them with Ileana and their pattern was always the same. I would rise early and take my breakfast in the dining room of the Pine. As soon as her mother, Stefania, had liberated Ileana from her kitchen duties, we would go for a walk. Usually, we took the path by the stream but sometimes we ventured up through the fir trees, climbing into fresher, cooler air. Ileana was surprisingly hardy – people who live in the mountains usually are. Her long dress restricted her movements. But this was a blessing since it gave me a frequent excuse to lift her over an obstacle.

Her skill in acquiring English was astonishing. In fact, she put me to shame. I was attempting, under her tutelage, to learn Romanian and writing the words and phrases that she taught me in a notebook. However, her progress was far quicker than mine. By the end of the week, we were broaching, mainly in English, our deepest feelings. I divined from Ileana that she felt cramped and limited by her life here and that she was anxious to liberate herself from the prejudices and superstitions of the village. Ileana's mother felt that she was growing too old for the demands of the inn. She had dropped hints that Ileana should take over. But her daughter had no desire to do so. And it was unlikely that Radu, who was studying in Bucharest, would assume the role.

On a Saturday morning in late August, I was sitting at my accustomed table in the Pine. It was to be a swelteringly hot day. I had almost grown accustomed to mamaliga now – it seemed there was little alternative to eating it at this hour. Ileana's mother, Stefania, attempted to make the dish more palatable by giving me glasses of a strong, home-made spirit, called tuica. It made one's eyes water. She found it hard to grasp the concept that I did not wish to become intoxicated at eight o'clock in the morning.

In general, I felt fitter than I had for years. Regular exercise and the clean air of the village had done me the world of good. Only one thing was troubling me – the fact that I would soon have to go home. Today, I would broach the subject with Ileana. It was fortunate that before leaving England I had stitched four gold sovereigns into the lining of my Norfolk jacket. I hoped that I should be able to exchange these for local currencies.

As it happened, fate decided my course of action. I had just finished my meal, when Radu came into the room. He was carrying a newspaper. He placed it carefully on the table. It was the *Daily Mail* – an edition from the 4th of August. The first thing I saw was an emphatic headline: GREAT BRITAIN DECLARES WAR ON GERMANY.

My eyes skipped down a dense column of newsprint.

"Owing to the summary rejection made by the German Government of requests made by His Majesty's Government ... a state of war exists between Great Britain and Germany ..."

Of course, I had been vaguely aware of the events earlier in the summer – the assassination of the Archduke at the end of June, the Austrian ultimatum to the Serbs and the mobilisations of the European and Russian armies. In reality, the denouement – Britain, France and Russia squared up against Germany and its allies had been almost inevitable.

"The newspaper arrived this morning, with some letters," Radu explained. "It is old, I think."

"Yes, two weeks."

"You must leave for England."

"Of course. What will happen here?"

Radu shrugged.

"Dumbrava is a sleepy place. Who knows?"

"What will you do?" I said.

"I shall contact the university and ask their advice. And

you?"

"I suppose that I must leave straight away, perhaps tomorrow."

"You cannot," said Radu.

"Sorry?"

He explained that a feast had been organised and that I was the guest of honour. It was to be held at the inn. The following morning, Vasile would take me to Kolozsvar. He suggested, in the circumstance, that I travel home through Bulgaria, crossing the Black Sea to Constantinople. From there, I would be able to take a steamer to England.

"I see." I had not intended to follow my father's route of fifty years before, back to England through the Dardanelles. I was touched that Radu had planned my itinerary.

"I had not planned to go that way," I said.

"I think that there is no alternative." He looked at me. "It is a pity that we must both leave, in these circumstances. But at least we may be on the same side. From what I have read of our new king, Romania may not side with Germany."

"Perhaps the war will be over quickly," I said, trying to lighten the mood. "I am looking forward to showing you my house, and my city, Radu. We will drink porter and eat roast beef. We will take a tram down to Piccadilly Circus. And we will go to a music hall."

"Thank you, Mr Endicott."

"Would you like a drink?"

Radu looked down at my small glass and wrinkled his nose. He declined. He did not like tuica.

The following night. Vasile, Radu and I shared a rough bench in the Pine. It was a balmy night and the sky was thickly clustered with stars. The inn was lit by guttering lamps. Like my club in London, its yellow walls had absorbed decades of smoke and laughter. The noise inside was deafening. The whole village seemed to be here. We had eaten a copious meal of tripe soup, followed by succulent pork with sour cream. Tankards had been raised and backs thumped. We had congratulated each other upon our defeat of the German army. Vasile, the blacksmith, had embarked upon a long speech, in honour of the brave Englishman. He had grasped me by the shoulders with tears moistening his dark eyes and embraced me. It was terribly embarrassing. We had all mourned Florin. His absence from the feast was palpable.

As the food settled in our bellies we downed, with increasing recklessness, small glasses of tuica. Now, tears of laughter mingled with tears of sadness. The inn became a blur to me. The laughter and conversation congealed into a haze. Each time Ileana came to bring a new dish or to clear the table our eyes met. Drink had emboldened me and had given an urgency to my feelings. But a more rational voice – it was that of my brother Godfrey – had been pouring cold water over my head. People do not fall in love with complete strangers, the voice told me. The heart is merely a pumping muscle. I found this jeremiad reassuring. For whenever Godfrey told me not to do something, I knew that I was on the right track.

"To Sherlock Holmes!"

We had already toasted King George V, King Carol and the Romanian army.

"To Sherlock Holmes!"

Radu's eyes were blazing as he downed his small glass at a single gulp.

Now was the time for music. On the other side of the room was a small gypsy orchestra. Its violinist began a rumbustious melody, beating time with his foot. The tune had an Asian flavour but there was enough of a jig or reel in it to awaken my long dormant rhythmical instincts. The heavy tables were pushed aside to clear a space in the centre of the floor. To my mortification, Vasile, his face as ruddy as a beetroot, took my arm. I, the Englishman, was his most honoured guest. He insisted that I join the villagers in one their traditional dance, the *hora*.

Fortunately, I was recklessly drunk. The villagers formed themselves into a large circle. They were holding hands while lifting and lowering their arms. I soon got into the spirit of the thing. Nobody seemed to notice my clumsiness. It was a joyous occasion – a moment of comradeship and elation. I knew that Vasile would risk his life for me, and I for him, and that we would retain these feelings, even when our heads were no longer sore.

More dances followed. Even Radu, who was a sensible young man, had now become glassy-eyed. The pace slowed. The young men of the village now shyly approached village maidens and matriarchs paired off with grizzled old farmers. I noticed that Ileana was standing by the back wall. She was wearing her best white dress, with a colourful apron. I had never seen anyone more beautiful.

Hands seemed to push into the small of my back and propel me across the room. Soon, I was looking straight into her eyes. I took Ileana's her hand and we began to dance. It was a slow dance, at least by the standards of Dumbrava de Sus, and it compelled me to place my hands on her waist. I can barely describe the feelings that touching Ileana aroused in me. The movements we must make were relatively simple and she guided my fumbling steps. The villagers seemed delighted that we were together. They clapped and cheered us on.

There is a moment at every wedding feast when the musicians are tired but continue to indulge the last few couples on the floor. There is always a last couple, welded together in a circle of light. And there is always a moment when the last couple retires into the private darkness. Ileana took my hands. She looked up at me, her eyes wide and bright. She led me outside. The air smelt of hay and warm, ripe fruit, for it was harvest time. We looked up at the sky.

"Cassiopeia," said Ileana. I was overjoyed that knew the same word for the same thing. The W-shaped constellation was almost directly above us. My father had shown me the major constellations, when I was little. I began to point out to her the plough and the pole star. I surprised myself then. I pulled her body to face me. Soon, I was enjoying her hot passionate kisses. I never wanted to stop. The kiss had sealed our fate.

The following morning, Ileana watched solemnly as I packed a few things into my remaining suitcase. We had promised to exchange letters and said that we would not be sad when we parted. I felt ravaged by tiredness. I clicked the lid of the leather case shut and looked around the small room. It had become my home. I had almost forgotten my other life.

"Austin ..."

She moved forwards. I drew her towards me. We embraced. She moaned softly as I moved my hand down her back.

"I am so sorry that I must go," I said. "I will return here, as soon as I can. And one day I will show you London. I promise"

Downstairs, I was presented me with a parcel of delicious food by Stefania. There was a game pie, some ripe peaches and a bottle of murfatlar, a bracing red wine. Vasile was waiting outside, in his pony and trap. From Kolozsvar, I would take the coach to the Saxon town of Szeben to the south. Then I would head through the Transylvanian Alps. The sky was cloudless and the sun burned one's back.

Before we had reached the end of the village street, I glanced back. I would always remember the village – its stone houses with untidy storks nests on their chimneys; the church with its wooden spire; the circular hay ricks; the fragrant smell

66

of smoke. Ileana stood out like a small white doll. She gave a wave. I knew that she would watch the pony and trap until it had rounded the corner. I hoped that she would not cry too much.

Chapter Seven

The journey home was long and arduous. I shan't detain you with the details – my interminable dealings with Romanian customs officials (I had to bribe them with one of the sovereigns); the long slow crawl over the brown plains of Wallachia; my distressing experiences in Bulgaria. In the Black Sea port of Vanu, I boarded an indescribably filthy ship, which I shared with itinerant workers and their animals. There were no cabins; we were merely huddled on the deck beneath a tarpaulin. It was an uncomfortable night, but I shall never forget its conclusion.

Dawn came. The stars faded and I watched, fascinated, as the minareted skyline of Constantinople grew closer. I saw the great dome of the blue mosque, with a thin sliver of moon just above it. As the ship entered the mouth of the Bosphorus, we heard the plangent cry of a muezzin calling the faithful to prayer. The water was silver. The exciting city, with its strange sounds and smells, swallowed up the little vessel. It was a human rabbit warren, teeming with secrets and mystery; a real metropolis, as thrilling and stupendous as London, but redolent of Asia and the spice routes.

On the dock, was a telegraph office. And here I dispatched a telegram to Harry, at the *Evening News* in Fleet Street. I wanted to get his attention and, constrained by finance, composed a short, graphic message: "Dear Harry, returning from Dumbrava de Sus. Believe Germans making secret bomb on Devil's Mountain. However, mine destroyed! London in five days."

It was a huge mistake. Sending that telegram was extremely naive. I now know that before it arrived at the *Evening News*, many other people had considered its contents. The three sentences would first have been puzzled over by some clerk at the central telegraph office at St. Paul's. They would then have been referred to the Home Section of the Secret Service Bureau, or MI5, and, from there, passed to Special Branch. Special Branch would have telegraphed P & O's offices in Constantinople and requested the physical description and travel itinerary of a passenger called Austin J. Endicott, so that they could pick him up in England.

My third class cabin in the P & O steamer the *Osiris* was plainly furnished but reasonably comfortable. The sea journey was a good chance to rest my body, which was still aching in various places, to take regular meals and to refresh my journal. On early mornings, watching birds wheeling over the ship's wake, I had a curious feeling that my father was watching me and was trying to tell me something. But what?

After the Straits of Gibralter, I was in a hurry to get back to England. I knew that the country would be buzzing with the war and that the tom-toms of the press would be beating fast but the sight of the white cliffs and the emerald grass of Dover were strangely reassuring. I was missing Ileana desperately and had composed numerous notes to her in simple English in my cabin. My mind was full of conflicting thoughts as we docked. What would the war be like? How and when would I see Ileana again? I had no answer to either question and, of course, I could not know what was about to happen. As soon as I set foot in Dover, I was picked up by the police!

Loudly protesting that I was innocent of any crime, I was frog-marched by two uniformed constables to the dirtiest, dingiest part of the dock. Here, in an airless room, a plain-clothed officer was already waiting. It was my first encounter with a Special Branch officer.

Inspector Gribley was wearing a black pin-striped suit, with a matching waistcoat, and a white shirt with a shiny celluloid collar. In the middle of Blackfriars Bridge, he would have been entirely inconspicuous; here, he cut a strange figure. I asked to see his warrant card. With a heavy sigh, stale with tobacco, he produced it.

"Let's get straight to the point, shall we?"

Gribley had small grey eyes, which became animated when he was excited, and a dimpled chin.

"This telegram."

He tapped the document with his finger.

I shrugged.

"Bomb. Devil's Mountain?" said Gribley.

"That's what it says."

"What does it mean?"

"You do speak English ..." I am not normally sarcastic but the vicissitudes of the past few days had hardened me.

"Right!"

Gribley turned nimbly, like a ballroom dancer. He squatted close to me, so that his furrowed brow was inches from my face. His breath was rank.

"Don't be clever my lad! Do you know why?" He glared at me. "I am seriously considering arresting you, as a spy. If that happens, and you are found guilty, you are going to hang. Do you understand? Now, let's start again."

Gribley stood back, glowering like an angry terrier.

I sighed. I might as well tell him the whole story.

"Very well," I said. "I have been in the Apuseni mountains, in the Hungarian province of Transylvania. Many years ago, my father was there ..."

I went through whole tale, only omitting only scenic descriptions. Gribley listened to me carefully. As I spoke, he loaded his pipe, firmed the tobacco in the bowl with his thumb and lit up with one match, filling the room with aromatic smoke. The smell reminded me of my father's study.

I described the hedonite mine, the barracks in which the slave workers lived and the extent of the German military presence on the mountain. I explained how I had camped in a cave with villagers from Dumbrava de Sus and that the mine and its workings had been destroyed (I did not give the precise details). I then backtracked to Broadhurst – the man who had first alerted me to the mountain. I suggested to Gribley that Broadhurst had been murdered by a German secret agent. Gribley failed to react. Perhaps he had been trained not to betray emotion while interrogating, or perhaps the accusation was of no interest to him.

"This 'secret bomb'," he pronounced the words with a kind of sneer. "What do you think it is, exactly?"

I looked at him. "I do not know. I assume that there is some explosive property in hedonite and that when it is aggregated in a sufficient quantity ..."

He breathed a stream of blue smoke through his nostrils. I felt sorry for him. I mean, it was not a normal police matter, like stolen silverware or a speeding motor. The story was a conflation of a Grimm's fairy tale and an implausible scientific fable.

"I see," he said, cutting me off. "Wait here."

What did he think I was going to do? Launch myself through the window and make a dash for it? Gribley left me in the custody of a police constable and went into an adjoining room. I then heard a muffled telephone conversation. Did Special Branch already know about the hedonite mine and the Germans' plans? Perhaps Gribley merely thought I was mad. In which case, I would be lucky not to be carted off to the nearest lunatic asylum.

The detective came back into the room.

"You can go," he said.

"I beg your pardon?"

"I have looked into the matter and I am satisfied that, under the terms of the Defence of the Realm Act, you do not, at this time, represent a threat to the security of the United Kingdom. However, I must warn you that from henceforth you will be under the surveillance of the authorities and that should you behave in a treasonable or seditious manner ..."

Outside, it was raining. It is always raining in Dover. One of the constables handed me my suitcase. I later discovered that it been thoroughly searched. The silk lining of the case had been cut neatly with a razor blade. The rain was refreshing. The constable was a local man with a round face.

"Sorry about that, but we do have to be careful sir, what with the war. You can't trust anybody these days. Now, let's get you to the station."

He smiled at me. His ruddy cheeks were glowing. It is only in England, I reflected, that policemen rescue cats from trees and are reluctant to carry firearms. I followed the constable down a long, cobbled street to a taxi stand. From there, I took a cab to Dover station.

It seemed like several years since I had last been at London Bridge station, instead of a few weeks. But the world was utterly different. Each newspaper and casual conversation told the same story. Our lads, the British Expeditionary Force, had sailed for France and were already engaging with the enemy. They would give the Huns a bloody nose, that was the general view, and our dreadnoughts would knock spots off the German fleet in the North Sea. Our brave boys would return to tell of their heroic exploits, "before Christmas". I knew that German, Austrian and Hungarian newspapers were serving up their readers the same cheerful twaddle. Soon, the humiliating retreat from Mons would change the country's mood. The optimism of the flags and bunting that bedecked the streets would come to appear incongruous.

I arrived in London in the early evening. Although it was nearly dark and I was desperately tired, I decided to pop back to the office, to check my affairs. Floyd had gone home; there was no-one about. The first thing I noticed was that my chair was facing the wrong way; the second was that the safe door was open. There was no conceivable reason why this should be so. I had left this room locked when I had left, and only Floyd had the key. I checked the safe. The accounts, the deeds to the shop and some other personal papers were intact. Only one thing was missing – the Blood Stone.

Over the next few weeks, Gribley's words came back to haunt me: "From henceforth, you will be under the surveillance of the authorities." He was right. Virtually every item of incoming mail that bore my name had been opened and crudely re-sealed. A fellow appeared outside. He became a permanent fixture in the cafe opposite the Exhibition Rooms. He was an anonymous character in a dark suit and a bowler, a kind of uber-Gribley. Special Branch clearly wished me know to know that they were prying into every aspect of my life.

The scrutiny of my life continued into September. I had written to Ileana in Dumbrava de Sus and to Radu in Bucharest several times but had received no reply. I had explained that I would return to Transylvania "as soon as possible". But I had no idea when this would be. Actually, I was wondering whether to sell the Exhibition Rooms and move on. People no longer seemed to be interested in their mixture of sensationalism and anthropology. The business had declined catastrophically over the previous year. But what was I to do? My Oxford degree was in classical languages. I was not equipped for any career or profession that I could think of.

One morning in October, I was sitting disconsolately in my office. It was half past nine. Floyd was downstairs, unpacking some crates of war clubs and wooden fetishes from the Congo. I knew that I should be helping him. I was marking time by idly flicking through a copy of a local newspaper, the *Hampstead and Highgate Express*. That's when I saw the photograph.

It had attracted my curiosity, because it showed a member of the royal family, David, the Prince of Wales, and such elevated personages rarely appeared in the pages of the *Ham & High*. The young prince seemed in a serious mood. The wind had tousled his hair. He was standing next to a man with a moustache dressed in a military uniform – a tunic with an upturned collar and a peaked cap. They were stiffly shaking hands.

Suddenly, I noticed something. On each side of the officer's collar was an insignia. It looked like a star. I took a magnifying glass from my desk to have closer look. I now saw that the stars were winged.

My heart skipped a beat. The markings were the same as those on the jacket of the German who had tried to steal the Blood Stone from the Exhibition Rooms back in April! Beneath the photograph was a caption: "His Royal Highness David, Prince of Wales, is shown on a recent visit to Minerva House, Highgate. His Majesty was received by Brigadier Thomas Eyre Hinton, honorary president of the Minerva League."

The brigadier was smiling almost indiscernibly in the picture, obviously thrilled by his proximity to a member of the royal family. What was the Minerva League, I wondered? And why on earth was the Prince of Wales associated with the same organisation as a German assassin?

By coincidence, I had arranged to meet Harry Hawkins for a drink that night, after his paper had gone to press. To his disappointment, my return from Transylvania had not led to the photograph, and the story, that he had hoped for. Admittedly, I had found a slave mine, and it had been destroyed. But there was no evidence that it had ever existed. As to the dragon that I had seen emerging from a lake of lava – Harry simply did not believe me. He asked me if I drunk too much of the local fire water.

My friend kept late hours. He arrived out of breath and soaked, saying that it was raining cats and dogs outside. My club, the Travellers', was a cosy, old-fashioned establishment, located off Regent Street, only ten minutes walk from the Exhibition Rooms. My father had been a member too – he had sat on these very leather chairs and studied the same battered volumes of Thucydides and Virgil. His exploits were ingrained in the clubs' annals. I had a lot of catching up to do. But the staff were unfailingly polite to me, like the loyal retainers of some old English dynasty.

We sat in the library, before a blazing fire, as Harry slowly dried off. There was a gramophone in the adjoining smoking room. It had been playing some Viennese waltzes. But an indignant old fossil had complained that they were "unpatriotic", so the music had been stopped. Now, a hum of conversation was the only backdrop. Steam was rising from Harry's trousers.

In the last few minutes, I had told my friend that I was being followed by a little man in a bowler and that my post was being opened. I had also described the intriguing photograph I had seen that morning in the *Ham & High*.

Harry rolled warm amber liquid around in his glass. He was a whisky man. I usually drank brandy, or hoc and seltzer if my liver was a bit queasy.

"It's all very queer," he said

"This Minerva League," I said, "have you ever run into it, Harry?"

He shook his head.

"The fact is," he said, "there is really only one way to find out about it."

"And what is that?"

He gave me a firm look.

"By becoming a member."

"I'm sorry?"

"One of us, you or I, must join the Minerva League and ask some searching questions."

"That is easy for you to say," I replied.

There was pause. "Wasn't going to Transylvania my idea?" said Harry.

"Yes," I said, "and look what happened ... I was almost killed by German soldiers, I crossed a fiery abyss on a bridge made out of string, I watched a boy die, " I paused for breath. "And, by the way, we have achieved nothing."

"But you have fallen in love." Harry always knew my weak points.

"Yes, there is that."

A waiter came into the library, carrying a tray.

Neither of us spoke. Thoughts raced through my brain. Was I going to give up now, after having travelled so far? Broadhurst had been survived by a son who was serving in the Royal Navy. I had never met the lad, but I certainly owed him something.

"I suppose you are right," I said, slowly. "If we can find out what the Minerva League is, it may take us closer to the German officer and to the significance of the Devil's Mountain. But how are we going to do it?"

Hawkins was in his element. He said that it would be relatively easy to infiltrate the league, especially for a public school man. Those whose lives were ruled by fantasy, like Brigadier Hinton, were always credulous.

Harry glanced at the waiter and then at his empty glass. "Drink?"

My friend, inevitably, was imbibing a venerable malt. It was the most expensive whisky in the club. I sighed.

"Very well," I said. "One for the road."

"That's the spirit!" Harry laughed.

The following morning, I addressed a short but fawning note, from my business address, to Brigadier Thomas Eyre Hinton, of Minerva House, Highgate. The letter said that I would be most interested to learn more about the Minerva League and implied that I was a very successful businessman, with well-connected friends.

The brigadier replied almost by return. His note was written in pencil, in a firm, neat hand. There was an intriguing symbol on the letterhead. It was the winged, five-pointed star that I had seen in the newspaper photograph. Two points of the star pointed upwards, like the horns of a goat.

The brigadier advised me that the Minerva League held regular public lectures. He had enclosed a small hand-bill. The title of the first talk made me shudder – *Eugenics: the Science of Social Hygiene* by Edgar Schuster. Other talks were devoted to theosophy, spiritualism and Vedic religions. The last was the most interesting – *Uranium: the Key to the World's Future*. The title meant little to me, for, at that time, I had no knowledge of the element and its extraordinary properties.

In his final paragraph, the brigadier invited me to a private event, a social evening and lecture, at his house. It was to be held the following Saturday. Guests would be wearing evening dress, he advised. I telephoned the brigadier's number immediately and told his servant that I should be delighted to accept.

Chapter Eight

I love motor cars and there were several interesting ones parked on the gravel drive in front of Minerva House. There was a lovely Bugatti T20, a sleek Mercedes Benz and, best of all, a white Rolls Royce Silver Cloud. A chauffeur was sitting in its driving seat. I said hello to him but he ignored me. It was a bad start to the evening. I was dressed in a silk-lapelled dinner jacket, with a white shirt and a black bow tie. I felt uncomfortable and rather nervous.

A man in a crimson dress tunic let me in. He was wearing tight black trousers and had a rolling gait. It looked as though his cheeks had been rouged. A blast of warmth came from an open door off the hallway. I gave the servant my card and he led me through. Later, I described the scene to Hawkins – knots of people clustered around the edges of a drawing room, the men in cummerbunds, the women in silk dresses, with tiaras and diamond earrings. There were self-important old men with pince-nez and side whiskers; serious looking young men with watery eyes and scarred cheeks. I recognised the music as the overture to *Parsifal* by Wagner. I have always disliked the pomposity of Wagner and his mythological hokum. I began to bristle from the inside. Weren't we supposed to be at war with ...

"Serena ..." a pale-faced man with a black beard rudely brushed passed me. He scrutinised my face, then dismissed me. "I must introduce you to the Austrian vice consul ..." A tall, thin woman in a white dress followed in his wake.

A solitary guest standing a little way off was staring at me. He had a long nose and the cruel eyes of a kitten torturer. He was an unappealing character; I made a mental note to give him a wide berth. A ripple of anticipation passed through the room as Brigadier Hinton entered. The man's olive drab jacket had a colourful strip of medal-ribbons. He was quite short. His figure indicated social standing, good manners, and discipline, from his highly polished riding boots to his neatly-trimmed moustache. From my position on the other side of the room I could just distinguish the five-pointed star on his collar. The brigadier stood in front of a lectern. One sensed that he was used to addressing large groups of people.

"Your Royal Highness, Count von Buttolph, Mr Ambassador, ladies and gentlemen." It was a well-bred voice, like that of a squire at a fox hunt.

"You are very welcome to this lecture and to ... ahem ...." his sentence jerked off course, as if a gramophone needled had skipped off its groove. Most old soldiers have nervous tics. "... my home."

A sigh passed through the room as he successfully completed his sentence. "This is a proud moment, for me, and for the ... ahem ... Minerva League." His voice grew softer. "We are here to honour the founding fathers of our great movement – His Royal Highness, the Count, Sir James Folie, the Marquess of Abergavenny. I cannot ... ahem ... name them all."

An immensely dignified man close by twitched slightly, as if he had been slighted. He could barely stand, bedecked as he was with medals, orders and gold braid, like an over-garnished Christmas tree. The man's blue uniform was complemented by his red face and snow white hair. He must be the king of somewhere at the very least.

"Tonight, we may justifiably celebrate our successes. The war has started and soon, please God, may it reach a definitive and successful conclusion."

"Here here!" It was the rude fellow with the beard, who had cut me dead. His affirmation sailed through the drawing room, but landed flat, like a punctured tennis ball.

The brigadier continued. "But, as well as celebrating, we are also here to listen. The subject of the talk this evening is that which has brought us together. It is that which makes our project possible; that which, like a beacon, illuminates the way ahead."

"However," his face twitched, "I must not trespass upon the subject of our eminent speaker, Mr Lawrence Redfern of the Normal School of Science in Kensington."

He paused. "Before we begin, I have one small but pleasant duty to perform."

The brigadier's bright eyes darted around the room. In the last few minutes, the red-coated servant had been filling people's glasses. The brigadier raised his arm.

"Your Royal Highness, Count von Buttolph, Mr Ambassador, ladies and gentlemen ... I give you ... ahem ... the Kaiser!"

"The Kaiser!"

The syllables echoed around the drawing room, accompanied by the sound of snapping heels. I must admit, I was astonished. A kind of rage began to swell up inside me. Breathe Austin, I heard an interior voice say. Breathe slowly. You must remain calm. My glass was empty when it touched my lips. I had already tipped its sickly contents onto the carpet.

After the toast, the dignitaries were invited to sit on plush velvet seats ranged in front of the lectern. The rest of us had to stand behind them. Lawrence Redfern was a confident speaker. He was a tall man with long, pale hair, wearing a soft collar and a paisley tie. There was something of the fop about him, but he appeared to be well-versed his chosen subject. I have retained a strong visual impression of his yellow hair , his pink fleshy face and his breathless delivery. Fishburn held up for our examination a glass bottle with a cork stopper.

"Do you know what this is?" He did not wait for a reply.

"It is pitchblende, or uranium oxide. This small bottle holds about half a pint. Dull isn't it?"

He held up the bottle again.

"It looks unexciting ladies and gentleman. But, I can confidently predict, that the contents of this bottle are set to change, utterly, everything that we, the human race, have ever known. Why?" His eyes flashed. "Because locked into its atoms is a virtually limitless supply of energy. Those of you who have read Mr Wells' new book, *The World Set Free* will know that one pound or uranium contains as much energy as three million pounds of coal! Three million pounds!

"This little bottle alone, ladies and gentleman, is the equivalent of eighty tons of coal. Imagine, if you will, unlimited heat, light and power for the human race, for as long as we occupy this planet. Imagine, cities of white towers stretching to horizon, blazing with light. Imagine ships as tall as mountains that can sail around the world without refuelling. Imagine, if you will, a world, as Mr Wells has predicted, a world set free. That is not a fanciful supposition; it is the potential contained behind this glass."

The bottle was vibrating in his excited grasp. For a moment, I feared that he would drop it, with disastrous consequences for Highgate. Redfern replaced the object on the lectern.

"We know from the experiments of Mr Rutherford in Cambridge, that uranium merely consists of electrons orbiting a nucleus and that, in this form, it is stable."

I felt myself becoming bored. The rancid tang of the laboratory, with its test tubes and Bunsen burners seemed to assail my nostrils. I had hated chemistry at school

"But imagine this!" He stared into the bottle on the lectern. "What if there were a form of uranium whose energy could be unlocked through a simple physical process? And what if it this chemical occurred abundantly at a certain location within our own continent?

"Members of the Minerva League." Redfern's pupils were

strangely dilated. "I can tell you, tonight, that my words are no fantasy; that such a mineral has been discovered, in a quarry to the east, and, also, that through the sudden unleashing of its stupendous energy, it could win the war at a single stroke. I am talking, honoured guests, about the most powerful weapon that the world has ever seen. Even the threat of its use, after a suitable demonstration, would end the present conflict within hours. That is the prospect ahead of us, tonight – victory!" His blue eyes seemed to sparkle. "My fellow Minervans, I would like to propose a toast."

The redcoat had been replenishing glasses. What was on offer was not champagne but some sweet German wine.

"I give you," said Redfern, "the key to the world's future. Ladies and gentlemen," he paused for effect. "Uranium!"

The phrase bounced back at him.

"Uranium!"

After the toast, people began to leave. The dignitaries were steered decorously towards their motor cars. However, the evening was not finished, for the small orchestra that had been playing earlier was arranging itself at the end of the drawing room. Looking around, I felt that I had never seen such an unappealing group of people. I studied them – the cream of the Kaiser set, feasting on white wine and canapes. The orchestra began to tune up. I remembered the party in Dumbrava de Sus, with its gypsy musicians. How different that gathering had been to this and how happy I had felt that night.

The man with the large nose and cold eyes glanced in my direction again. I noticed, with alarm, that he was making his way towards me. Oh well. I took a deep breath.

His hand was as cold and clammy as clay.

"My name is Schuster, Edgar Schuster," he said. "And you are?"

I managed to free my hand. "Austin Endicott."

"You may be familiar with a book that I have written?" He

stared at me strangely. "It is called *Eugenics*."

Eugenics, the notion that the human race could only progress by eliminating the weak and unfit, for example through enforced sterilisation, was utterly abhorrent to me.

"Of course I have," I lied.

"Then you agree with my theories?"

"Agree with them? I have been proselytising on your behalf, all over London."

Schuster seemed to grow six inches taller.

"Not only do I agree with them," I said. "It is my belief that unless we control the current indiscriminate human breeding, our race is doomed to suffer extinction."

He chortled with glee. His hair was plastered unpleasantly over his head with grease – smearing the contents of a frying pan over his cranium would have acheived exactly the same effect. For the next ten minutes, Schuster, who was German, explained to me how the "germplasm" of the Anglo Saxon race had been compromised, for example through its contact with Negroes. I had to smile and nod my way through this rubbish, looking for a way to escape.

"... have you met Brigadier Hinton?"

My ears pricked up.

"I er ... no, I have corresponded with him, of course."

"Would you like to?"

He cocked his head to one side.

"He is a good friend of mine," Schuster explained. "Would you like me to introduce you?"

The prospect was about as appealing as being dosed with cod liver oil. But I could hardly refuse. Harry had once explained to me that, in his quests for truth there was always a "pay off". This was it.

"Could you really do me such a service?" I said, incredulously.

"Of course."

Schuster actually snapped his fingers. It was embarrassing. In response, the red-coated servant crossed the room. Some words were mumbled. I followed the two men across a tiled hallway.

Hinton's study was as stuffy and over-heated as an orchid house. An extravagant fire was burning in the hearth. The first thing I noticed, after the hot coals, was a large gramophone horn. The brigadier was seated by the fire. His face was flushed. He must have been drinking whisky.

"Edgar!" He raised himself unsteadily to his feet and extended a liver-spotted hand.

Schuster was gripping my arm. He thrust me forwards, as if I were some kind of trophy.

"This young man is dying to talk to you," he said.

"I am all ears."

There was a moment's silence. Laughter punctured our unease. Schuster's laugh sounded like the call of a hyena. I explained to Hinton, that, as I had said in my letter of introduction, I was in the importation businesses, mainly of African curios.

"Ah, Africa," said Hinton, interrupting my flow. "I have served there twice, you know." He tapped the ribbons on his chest. "Won my DSO at Ladysmith. Never under-estimate the Boer, Endicott. He's a splendid chap, as fierce as a ferret. Edgar here knows. He has kinsmen in the veldt, don't you Edgar?"

"I assure you, sir, that I would not ..."

"But the blackie, now, that's a different matter."

Hinton loved the sound of his own voice. This, of course, gave me an advantage. All I had to do was to dangle myself in front of him, like a succulent piece of bait, waiting for him to ensnare himself.

"When I was in the Congo ..."

Hinton embarked upon a long story, illustrating the untrustworthiness of the Negro. Treat him like a dog, and he will respect you, that was the gist of it. Schuster listened admiringly. While he was talking, I studied his face. It was brown and leathery. His eyes had been narrowed into slits by the fierce African sun.

"A Negro tried to join the Minerva League once, Endicott. Can you believe it?" He looked at me. "I said to him, the only way you can get into my house, my friend, is as a hunting trophy!"

He guffawed.

"What do you think of the league, Endicott?"

"I do not know, sir," I said, being truthful. "It seems very ..."

"That's right." He jabbed at the fire, with his poker. "There is a serious side to it, you know, Endicott. A very serious side."

"Oh yes."

A conspiratorial look passed between Hinton and Schuster.

"I can't tell you what that is, at this juncture," said the brigadier. "But I can say this. I like the cut of your jib, young man." He reached towards my leg. I winced as I felt his fingers palpate my thigh. It was horrible. "Within the league, there is, shall say, an inner group, an elite." He released his grip. I breathed out. "They are the chaps who run the show, as it were. Edgar here is a member of our knight's chapter. You will need the recommendation of an existing member to join, Endicott, But, with the support of our good friend here, well ..."

His expression said it all. A world of marvellous opportunity would open up for me.

"Bob's your uncle."

Schuster mouthed the phrase. He probably had no idea what it meant.

"I am truly honoured sir," I said, feeling my gorge rising.

Thank you."

He insisted that Schuster and I join him for a "wee dram". I did, telling myself that it was price worth paying. I have always disliked whisky. I could not get out of there quickly enough.

Chapter Nine

"It's a peculiar business," said Harry.

"It is indeed."

We were sitting, on a foggy November evening, in my club, in Charles II Street. The hour was late and the library had been abandoned save for us. We were cocooned in leather chairs, in front of a blazing fire. I had already recounted to Harry, in some detail, the events of the previous night. He had merely smiled when I had described the grisly members of the Minerva League – the odious Schuster, the bombastic dignitaries and the English Germanophiles, who had cheered the Kaiser to the rafters. I had also described Redfern's lecture and his apparent reference in his phrase, "in a quarry to the east", to the Transylvanian slave mine.

"I have never seen so many plumes and decorations," I told my friend, "and so many quivering jowls. It was like being in a room full of turkeys."

"And Brigadier Hinton?"

"What of him?"

My lip curled with distaste.

"What is he like?"

"He is short, rigid in bearing and incredibly pompous," I said.

"Did you speak to him personally?"

"Yes, of course."

"And ..."

Harry peered into my eyes.

I had no intention of telling him that Hinton had placed a hand on my thigh, while staring at me lasciviously. Some details were too embarrassing.

"Well," I said. "I was introduced to him by a horrible eugenicist. He lectured me on the superiority of the white man over the brown. He then intimated to me that I might be able to join the inner circle of the Minerva League – the knight's chapter, I think he called it."

"The knight's chapter."

"That is what I just said."

My friend laughed.

"How big is it?" he asked. "The knight's chapter I mean?"

He gazed thoughtfully into the fire.

"I have absolutely no idea. But, judging from the people I met in Minerva House, it has some pretty high-powered members."

"What happened then?"

"I said that I was immensely flattered to have been asked. I then made my excuses and left."

I looked at my friend. He had a sceptical expression on his face.

"I really don't think that I could have got any more out of Hinton," I said, "and, besides, I have not told you the best bit."

"What was that?"

"Well, I was walked to the front door with the eugenicist, Schuster, by Hinton's batman, Andrew. When I got there, I realised that I needed to ..."

"Answer the call of nature?"

"Exactly. The batman gave me directions. He was busy putting Schuster's coat on. I made my way down a tiled hallway to the back of the house. It was then that I made a mistake. Instead of turning left, as the batman had told me, I must have turned right. Something very strange then happened."

Harry leaned forwards.

"What was it?"

"I heard a moaning sound. It was a cross between chanting and the noise that the wind makes blowing through an old belfry. At the end of a corridor, was a set of double doors. They were paneled doors, painted maroon and green. The doors were partially open. I crept up to them and peered through."

"What did you see?"

My friend's eyebrow curled like an interrogation mark.

"This is the odd bit," I said. "You may not believe me, but I swear that everything I am telling you is the gospel truth." The coal fire flickered. Beads of red light danced on the surface of Harry's glass.

"It was a large room. But it was virtually full. I would say that there were about twenty men in there and a dozen or so women. Battle standards had been placed around the walls. Some of them bore the figure of a black raven."

Harry frowned. I continued.

"The men were wearing strange costumes – silver corselets and silk tunics. Some had Viking helmets. The men were chanting, while thumping their shields and spears on the floor. Forming an inner circle, as it were, with linked hands, were the women."

"How were they dressed?"

"They were kitted out as Viking maidens or Valkyries, like the chorus in a Wagner opera. They had white dresses, with scarlet bodices and blond hair tied into plaits. But the curious thing is ..."

"Yes?"

"Some of them were bare-breasted."

"Good lord."

My friends' eyes widened, like those of a startled owl.

"I know. I was shocked too."

"What were they doing?"

"The women were wailing in unison with the men, as if they were encouraging them, or egging them on. The room had a tiled floor, in a black and white checkered pattern, by the way. In the centre of the circle formed by the women was – you may not believe this Harry, but I swear it's true – a white goat. It was tethered by a rope to a metal ring. A man was standing behind the goat. And – do you know what – he was entirely naked, except for a small white apron, which barely covered his private parts!"

My friend did not say anything. I had, apparently, lost the capacity to shock him. He merely studied his whisky.

"He was not a handsome specimen. His skin was sallow and he had a sagging pot belly. The most remarkable things about him were his whiskers. The man had huge grey mutton chops. They swept out from each side of his face, like wings. He had a cruel, cunning expression. I shall never forget that."

"Did he? I mean was he ..."

"I don't know what he did to the goat, Harry," I said. "I dread to think."

My voice trailed away.

"What happened next?"

"I felt that I had seen enough. As you know, I hate cruelty to animals. I found the WC and made my way back to the front door. The batman gave me my coat, and I left."

The fire had died down to a crust of glowing embers. Both of our glasses were almost empty. I knew that Harry would want another drink, to "stiffen his sinews" as he would put it, for his cab ride back to Hampstead.

I rang a bell to call a waiter.

"Who do you suppose the man was, with the goat, I mean?" my friend said.

"I have no idea, Harry, I replied. An accountant, probably, or a bank manager, who knows? Whoever it was, I am sure that they are a pillar of the establishment."

"Quite so." Hawkins smiled. "Austin, you have done very well."

I warmed to my friend's compliment.

"Really?"

He nodded.

"Thank you."

"Shall we now examine the facts of the matter?"

"Let's."

He laced his fingers together, as if he were pondering a chess problem.

"First, we have a quarry or mine, which is located in Transylvania. The mine is, or was, until it was destroyed, in the gift of the Germans. As far as we are aware, the Germans are extracting uranium from the mine, so that they can make a bomb which would be a fantastically powerful weapon – more powerful than the world has ever seen."

I observed a gleam in my friend's eye. No doubt, some of these phrases would end up in one of his stories for the *Evening News*.

"Harry," I said, "I really don't think ..."

He silenced me.

"In the second place, we have a shadowy and rather unsavoury organisation, rivalling the Freemasons. It is called the Minerva League, after its meeting place. The league believes that the white race has been ordained by God to rule the earth. It is international in character and has members in the highest places, up to, and including, the British royal family!"

"Steady on, Harry," I said. "We don't actually know that, do we?"

"What about David, the Prince of Wales," my friend said. "We saw him in that photograph in the *Ham & High* did we not? Wasn't he shaking the hand of Brigadier Hinton?"

"Yes, he was," I said, "but that doesn't prove that the entire royal family ..."

"Austin," said my friend. "I am merely laying out the facts. We have the right to draw inferences from them, don't we? May I continue?"

"Of course," I said, "it's just that ..."

"Members of the Minerva League, with their riding crops and their tight jodhpurs, enjoy prancing around in each other's drawing rooms, toasting the Kaiser. They also like doing funny things with goats. But, in reality, they are extremely dangerous."

He looked at me.

"We know why, don't we Austin?"

"Tell me."

"They are dangerous because they may have in their hands a new and immensely destructive kind of armament. That means that our boys in the trenches may be sacrificing their lives for nothing. It may also mean ..." light from the dying fire glanced from his cheek, "that some of the most senior figures in Britain are traitors!"

"But Harry," I protested, "We don't know that the Germans are really developing such a bomb. And we don't know that the Minerva League ..."

"No, we don't." His jaw stiffened. "But, by God, we have to find out. It has become our duty to investigate the league and, if it is truly threatens our country, to destroy it."

"How on earth are we going to do that?"

"I have thought about that." He spoke softly. "We need to break into Brigadier Hinton's study in Minerva House and have a look around. Did he have a safe, Austin?"

"I can't remember," I said.

"I am sure that he does. Of course, we can't do this ourselves. But I know someone who can."

"Who is that?"

He looked evasive.

"All in good time, Austin. All in good time. Ah."

The waiter had arrived, offering the promise of two more drinks. I knew, from experience, that Harry could become as agitated as a high stepping colt when he was dilating upon a social evil. But his attention span was short. With the first sip of his whisky, he would probably have moved on to something else – the horrors of the white slave trade, or the fate of the Armenians. Usually, it was up to me to deal with the practical details of his moral crusades, or to remind him in the morning what he had been fulminating about the previous night.

I don't know if you are familiar with the narrow thoroughfares of Whitechapel? It seemed to me, on a dark, wet night the following week, that they had changed little since the days of Jack the Ripper. History seems to ooze from the walls. One can hear, in one's imagination, the cries and lamentations of Jews and Huguenots, of Irish peasants and of Russian Cossacks, transposed from their verdant homelands to this claustrophobic world of malodorous alleyways and ill-lit yards.

Wrapped up in long coats to disguise our social origins, Harry and I had drunk some lamentable spirits in a public house called the Ten Bells in Commercial Street. The place is little more than a large room, with gaudy tiled walls. Down one side is a long bar, backed by a mirror with frosted curlicues. Screeching harlots, sozzled lightermen and belligerent costermongers had cursed and fought in this arena for centuries.

It was early evening and a sulphurous darkness had insinuated itself through the streets. As the night progressed, the Bells would become even rougher. I checked the level of Harry's whisky, to assess how much longer we must stay. At least two of Jack the Ripper's victims, Annie Chapman and Mary Kelly, had supped gin in this very establishment before being butchered. This thought did not lighten my mood.

"When we get there, let me do the talking, Austin," mumbled Harry. "We don't want to get into any trouble and, after all, I do know this turf."

I sighed. Harry had just described, graphically, his

exposure of a Chinese opium den down in the East End docks, the previous year.

"Drink up," I said. A shaven-headed giant with scarred cheeks was eyeing us up from the other end of the bar. It could only be a matter of time before he challenged our manliness.

"Very well."

Harry knocked back his whisky.

"Come on then," he said.

If my friend had any knowledge of the geography of the East End, it had entirely deserted him in the past half-hour. It was I who steered us in the correct direction towards our destination, an address in Fournier Street. Even electric light struggled to illuminate the narrow road, which smelled of cabbages and blocked drains. A peeling green door led directly from the pavement. After flourishing a piece of paper, bearing a pencilled name, we were led, begrudgingly, up a flight of creaking stairs by the irascible mistress of the lodging house.

Harry rapped lightly on the door. He looked nervous. It opened.

"Sammy, my dear fellow."

The man was neither friendly nor unfriendly. After looking us up and down, he shook our hands and ushered us inside. At his invitation, we removed our hats and coats. We sat down at a table. It was covered by a grey cloth, bearing the ravages of numerous meals. Our host was dressed in a smart black suit, but wore no collar. This and his bristle-shadowed face gave him an aura of criminality. I looked around. In the East End, thruppence a week bought you a room whose walls were splattered with dead bugs, some broken furniture and an arthritic iron bedstead. I gained the impression that another man, now absent, also occupied this space.

"Drink, Mr 'Awkins?"

Harry smiled, falsely.

"We would love one."

The man reached into a wardrobe. Its door was hanging from a broken hinge.

My friend turned towards me.

"Sammy, and I am sure he will not mind me saying this, is one of the best safe crackers this side of the Mile End road. If not the best. Ain't you mate?"

The man shrugged.

"He is more familiar with the jewellers of Hatton Garden than are the employees of the Post Office."

Our host frowned. Harry realised that his compliment had been a little too specific.

"Allegedly!"

Uneasy laughter filled the room.

"He can pick any lock, blindfolded – that's why they call him Sammy the Shim. And he can scale drainpipes like a squirrel. I ran into Sammy when I wrote that story about Princess Mary's necklace. When was that? Back in 1912 wasn't it?"

The man looked blank. He poured a brackish looking liquid into three greasy tumblers.

"Now, don't get me wrong, Sammy is as straight as a die now, aren't you?" Harry winked. "But, occasionally, I, that is to say, we, use him on little jobs, when the investigations of the *Evening News* are being impeded. And this, I would say, is just such a case. By the way Sammy, I did not properly introduce my friend here, Austin Endicott. He sells curios, over in Bloomsbury."

I was not pleased that Harry had identified both my address and my occupation to a criminal. Sometimes, he could be an idiot.

The safe cracker extended his hand languidly for a second shake. He had long delicate fingers, their tips stained by nicotine. In a different world, he might have been a concert pianist. His face was pallid. His eyes, although I hesitate to use

95

such a trite expression, looked shifty.

"I should like to propose a toast."

Harry raised his filthy glass. Who were we going to drink to? Lord Northcliffe? The British Expeditionary Force? Charlie Chaplin?

"Gentlemen! To the success of our endeavours and to the elimination of the Minerva League."

It was midnight before we had finished. I would not say that I was drunk; rather that I had been poisoned by the filthy stuff that lived in the bottom of Sammy the Shim's wardrobe. It took me several days to recover. My role in the meeting was merely to explain to the East End thief the exact layout of Minerva House, in order to facilitate a break-in. In a few days, Sammy would reveal what he had found, in return for an agreed sum, paid from Harry's generous expenses.

Dealing with thieves, I have discovered, is rarely straight-forward. This is because they are intrinsically devious. Arrangements for the break-in, and for Sammy's remuneration, were sketched out, considered, abandoned and re-elaborated in great detail. However, by the time we had finished, we were the best friends in the world. We were "part-ners in crime", conjoined by a spurious friendship induced by drunkenness. The cheap whisky had taken its toll. As we made our way down Fournier Street, looking for a cab, my head was already aching, as if it were being pounded from the inside by a malevolent troll.

Chapter Ten

"Would you like to hear some good news, Austin?" asked Harry.

It was not a difficult question. I had a raging headache on account of drinking far too much with my friend the night before, in a foolhardy peregrination across Soho. We had been accompanied by Harry's companion of the moment, the actress Katie Kidd. As usual, when my friend was involved, the evening had been devoted to reckless excess.

"Yes, good news, please," I said.

Harry looked around suspiciously. We were sitting in a cafe in the shadow of the British Museum. The place was almost dark, although it was ten o'clock in the morning. It was crowded with workmen drinking mugs of white tea and eating fried breakfasts. Each time Harry glimpsed a man in a bowler through the rain-misted window he started – we had a strong suspicion that Special Branch was on our tail.

"Well," said Harry, "I am pleased to say that Sammy has come up trumps. He got into Minerva House and he managed to crack the safe. There wasn't much in it ... well there were a few things."

"What?" I snapped.

"There were details of bank accounts, there was some money – Sammy assures me that he did not take any of it – and there were membership records for the Minerva League. They make interesting reading. As well as the Prince of Wales, at least two members of the Cabinet and a clutch of MPs and Lords are on the list. I recognised a couple of chaps I was at university with."

"Won't Hinton be furious that you have stolen the list?"

"Of course, but what does it matter?"

I began to protest.

"Austin, we are above the law. We are acting in the public

interest. You must not think of it as a robbery."

"I suppose so, but even so ..."

"Sammy took quite a few letters from the safe. There were some letters to Franz Joseph, the king of Hungary, and to other dignitaries but by far the most significant was this."

He pulled something from his breast pocket.

"Can I see?"

He slid two sheets of paper across the stained table-top. They were carbon copies of a letter from Brigadier Hinton dated the 14th of February, 1914. The letter was addressed to Sir James Folie, FRS, of 63 Hargreave Mansions, Elizabeth Street, Westminster.

I scanned it.

"Dear Sir James," I read, *"I cannot thank you enough for your kind words and for the great support, both financial and moral, that you have given to the league. It is right that a movement like ours should grow organically by 'word of mouth'; you have done us a great service in commending our efforts to the Duke of ..."*

"Good Lord, Harry," I said, "this is tedious."

"Wait," said my friend. "You must look at the second page."

I did.

"... it is pleasing to report that Operation Siegfried is progressing well. A cargo vessel will be chartered to sail from the port of Hamburg to Alexandria in Egypt. In Alexandria, the cargo will transfer to a paddle steamer and progress down the Nile to Giza. My local contact, Mohamed, tells me that it is not uncommon for archaeological expeditions to follow this route and that it should attract little attention.

"Several hundred crates of mineral will be taken by camel train to the pyramid site. It is our best estimate that by September we will have mined enough for our task. In addition, in June or July, our friends in Bosnia have promised

to cook up a little scheme that will cause intense irritation, to say the least, to the Austrian Chancellor ..." I had reached the end of the sheet.

"How does the letter continue?" I asked.

Harry frowned. "I'm afraid that we don't have the third page. Sammy was in rather in a hurry when he bundled the papers into his bag. He must have come away without it."

"It's a shame," I said. I turned back to the first page. "Do we know who Sir James Folie is?"

"I do," said Hawkins, "because I looked him up this afternoon. He was formerly a professor of Egyptian and Oriental studies at King's College London. He is a member of the Athenaeum in Pall Mall. He lives in Belgravia."

"What do you suppose the letter means?"

My friend's eyes twinkled.

"I don't know," he said, "but perhaps ..."

"Perhaps what?"

"I'm guessing – it will require further research – that our friends in the Minerva League have come up with something really big. I think that they are planning to blow up a world-famous landmark," he paused, " the Pyramid of Cheops."

"I beg your pardon?"

"Think of it. The Great Pyramid is one of the most famous objects on the planet. If the league could turn it to dust, people would look and listen, would they not? Having accomplished this, the league could reveal that it had placed bombs in other places, such as London or Paris. Britain and her allies would be forced to surrender, immediately. We would have no choice but to accede to all of the league's demands, however outrageous."

"But surely," I began, "there may be other ..."

Harry brushed aside my objection. Once he had formed a hypothesis, he did not like it to be challenged. I tried another tack.

"Do you really think that this will happen?"

He reached into a pocket and produced a crumpled packet of Players. I was surprised. Normally, my friend only smoked when he was intoxicated, or under stress. He lit a match.

"I think that we may have been extremely fortunate, Austin."

"How is that?"

"You and your friends in Transylvania witnessed the destruction of the mine on the so-called Devil's Mountain in August, did you not? In doing so, you have deprived the Minerva League of the precious commodity upon which it depends – hedonite. Unwittingly, Austin, you may have saved Britain and her Empire. Would you like one?"

He offered me a cigarette. I declined.

"There was another interesting detail in the letter. Did you notice?"

"What was that?"

"Do you remember, Brigadier Hinton refers to 'our friends' in Bosnia?"

I nodded.

"Well, what if the league had organised the assassination of Archduke Ferdinand by Serbian anarchists?"

"It is possible, I suppose ..."

"It is more than possible," Austin. "The league wanted there to be a war, in order to demonstrate that it had the means to win it. It merely needed to light the touch paper. This letter is the evidence."

"Really? What do you suggest that we do now?"

My friend exhaled a cloud of acrid smoke.

"My dear Austin, I should have thought it was obvious. We must break into Sir James Folie's home, to see what we can find. We must do so as soon as possible – there is no time to spare. When we have the proof and I have written up my story for the *Evening News* we will submit a dossier of evidence to the Home Secretary and a copy to the Prime Minister."

"What will happen then?"

He paused.

"Either the leading members of the Minerva League will be clapped in irons – or we will be."

"Couldn't your friend Sammy do it," I said, "the break-in, I mean?"

He flicked his ash onto the floor.

"I'm afraid not. He is paid up for the last little job but I simply don't have enough money to finance another one – anyway, not on my expenses." He smiled curiously. "But don't worry, Austin." He had picked up the anxiety in my voice. "It will be easy. Folie lives in one of those mansion blocks off Buckingham Palace Road. If you have the right contacts, which I do, getting into them is a piece of cake. A child could do it. We'll just have a quick look round, when he is not there."

"We!"

"Of course we. You don't think I'm going to do this on my own, do you?"

He sounded shocked. Now he would try to butter me up.

"Look, Austin. I'm not asking you to climb over roof-tops or to jemmy a front door. All I need you to do is to act as a lookout."

"And to be an accomplice in a criminal act."

"Not a crime, more of a public service."

Harry fumbled for another cigarette and lit it. My friend was a man of extremes. He had changed in front of my eyes from a person who barely smoked to a tobacco addict.

I had crossed Europe, almost been killed, seen someone die and observed a semi-naked man cavorting with a goat, he reflected. Why should the small matter of committing a burglary bother me?

"When are we going to do this?"

He breathed out enough smoke to fill a kipper shed.

"Tonight. On Fridays, I have established, Folie does not return from Athenaeum until after eleven. I have obtained a pass key from the company which services his block."

Typical. He had made all the arrangements. Consulting me had merely been a formality.

"Do you have a pair of leather gloves?"

I nodded.

"And some dark-coloured unobtrusive clothing?"

"I thought that burglars wore striped jerseys and had false moustaches?"

He smiled again.

"Only in fiction, Austin."

The weather that Friday was filthy. I spent the afternoon in my office above the Exhibition Rooms, feeling apprehensive. Custom had dwindled to almost nothing; I wondered how long the business could stay open. Also, women were pursing their lips in the street as I passed them in the street. Why wasn't I in uniform, this signified. Sooner or later, I knew that I would probably join up. I was not a pacifist. However, for the time being, uncovering the seditious activities of the Minerva League seemed a greater moral imperative than serving in the armed forces.

At four o'clock, after he had brought my tea, I told Floyd to go home. There was nothing for him to do. By five, it was pitch dark. The wind was howling and rain was streaming down the windows. I was not to meet Harry until eight, in a public house in Pimlico. I can't remember the name of the establishment. We did not remove our hats or overcoats. We found a booth in a back room and downed a couple of drinks to give us Dutch courage. Harry was wearing a black Fedora, tipped over his eyes, and carrying a leather satchel. We tried to keep conversation to a minimum, in case anyone noticed us.

The actual burglary was ridiculously easy – or at least it appeared to be. I recall walking down a canyon-like street, feeling cold. The rain was driving against us almost horizontally. The mansion block had no concierge; we merely walked in, discovering a marble-floored hallway, and ascended to the third floor in an under-powered lift.

It was the kind of place where lords live while they are in town and where MPs keep their mistresses – clean, well-appointed but essentially anonymous. Hawkins moved noiselessly down the corridor ahead of me. The key worked perfectly. He did not pause or look round. In one movement, he opened the door and disappeared inside. I was to stand close to the door and tap on it three times, should danger approach. If anyone was curious as to why I was there, I would pretend to be making a delivery.

Harry had assured me that he would only be five minutes. But I knew that my friend had little awareness of time – this was one reason why normal avenues of employment were closed to him. Five minutes could actually mean fifteen, or even an hour. My career as a look-out was short-lived. After about two minutes of shifting my weight from foot to foot and feeling self-conscious, I looked down the corridor to see a horrifying sight. Two men were walking briskly towards me. They were wearing helmets and rain-capes. Policemen!

"Oh God!"

The corridor terminated in a dead-end. Our only escape would be to run past them and that was impossible. There was only one thing to do. I pushed the door, which Harry had left slightly ajar. As I did so, I heard heavy footfalls and the sounds of whistles. I closed the door from the inside. It was a stout one, but it would not hold them back for long.

"Harry! Harry!" I shouted.

I made my way down the hallway, which had a polished parquet floor. The study was ahead of me. I entered it. My eyes took in the salient details in a few seconds – a Persian carpet, dark wooden furniture, books, a roll-topped desk with papers spilling out. Harry must have levered it open. I heard voices.

"Open up! Open up in the name of the law!"

A policemen crashed against the door, like Thor's hammer. I knew that the game was up. I crossed the room. There was an open window above the desk. White curtains billowed into the room. There was a livid flash of lightning and a peal of thunder – the bulging clouds had discharged themselves. I leaned across the desk. Wind and rain lashed my face. A second lightning flash hit the building like an arc lamp. I looked down. Harry must have gone out through the window. But how? There was an inky void beneath. Where an earth had my friend disappeared to? Looking down, I could not even see the pavement.

As I pondered the enigma, a pair of pincers grabbed me around the waist. Soon, the breath of a large man was warming my face.

"Austin James Endicott?"

"Yes," I said, weakly.

"You are to come with us."

Chapter Eleven

I was bundled downstairs and thrust into a police car. Cuffed to a policeman I was pushed along the back seat. Someone was sitting there already. I recognised the reek of stale pipe tobacco mingling with a musty smell of leather and dust. It was my old adversary, Detective Inspector Gribley.

He looked me up and down.

"So you have taken to house breaking," he said sarcastically.

"There was a reason for it."

The cuffs were cutting into my wrist. I winced.

"Oh yes. What was that then?"

"Sir James Folie is a member of the Minerva League."

"The what?"

"The Minerva L ..."

"You young idiot!"

Gribley moved his face to within an inch of mine.

"Save this rubbish for later. I don't want to hear it."

My heart sank. I realised that Gribley would not listen sympathetically to anything I had to say.

"I warned you four months ago in Dover that should you continue in your seditious activities you would feel my hand upon your collar. You have chosen, for whatever reason, not to obey my warning and now, I am afraid, you must suffer the consequences."

"I am not a spy," I protested. "It is Sir Jamies Folie you should have arrested. He and leading members of the establishment are backing the Germans. They have developed a plan ..."

"Shut up!" he hissed. I breathed an aroma of stale tobacco, sweet hair oil and decaying teeth.

"I do not want to hear this nonsense, do you understand? I suggest, for your own sake, that you remain silent until we reach the station. Is that clear?"

I nodded glumly.

We were heading east and presently passed through Trafalgar Square and travelled up Charing Cross Road. Zeppelin raids had not yet made Londoners cautious. The pubs were full. Despite the wind and rain, men in toppers and long overcoats clustered around the brightly-lit theatres with silk-clad ladies. My stomach had contracted to a tight ball. I knew where we were going now – Bow Street.

I was 26 years old, and, strange as it may seem, I had never set foot in a police station. Gribley and the constable did not give me time to study the building's architecture. I was bundled roughly inside, like a murderer. A feeling of resignation had descended upon me in the car, like a heavy blanket. I sensed that I was passing into a world of darkness. It was true. And it would be more than a year before I would re-emerge into the light.

We stood in a gloomy room. Everything here was brown or grey and the walls were scratched and scuffed. Muffled sounds issued from the cells below. It was like the demon's grotto in a children's play. I was placed roughly on a mark in front of a custody sergeant. Gribley's mouth opened.

"I am arresting you under the Defence of the Realm Act. You do not have to say anything ..."

When he had finished the rigmarole of the caution, he pinched my forearm. He bent his head towards my ear.

"Spying is a capital offence, Endicott. I told you that in Dover, didn't I? And now, my lad, you are going to hang, as sure as eggs is eggs. We don't like traitors in this country."

The police constable, to whom I was still attached, grunted in assent.

"Take him downstairs."

Gribley turned away. I noticed that his shoes, sleek and highly polished, were like dancing pumps. I was led, or rather dragged, down a staircase that seemed to have been carved from granite into a dreadful and rebarbative underground kingdom. I lost a normal sense of time in the next few months. My life became determined, more than ever before, by mealtimes and other routines. The spaces between them seemed endless. I was in limbo.

The following morning, after the second most unpleasant night of my life (the worst had been when I was held captive in the Apuseni Mountains), I was formally charged and moved from Bow Street to Wandsworth Prison, to be held on remand. I was attached by leg-irons to a row of unsmiling felons in a "meat wagon". The poor fellow sitting next to me was shivering with fear. He was well-suited, like a superior artisan or a tailor and he was wearing a skull-cap. He was jabbering away in some Slavic language with a few words of Yiddish thrown in. Had he also been apprehended as a spy? I never found out.

What can I say about Wandsworth, except that I had now descended into the lower depths of Dante's inferno? As a prisoner one is denied the normal aspects of human identity. One is shorn of hair, dressed in itchy woollen clothes and addressed by number, rather than name – there are no "sirs" or "misters" in prison. My cell, which I was least spared the indignity of sharing, was about the size of a small scullery. It was equipped with a plank bed and a bucket for "slopping out". Here, I stared balefully as the walls in the prairies of time when I was not in the exercise yard, observed, periodically, through a spy-hole.

The other prisoners had been told that I was a traitor, which was somewhat lower in their typology of hatred than a man who abuses children. I went to sleep with their curses ringing in my ears. By a curious chance, this very cell had once been occupied by Mr Oscar Wilde, the playwright. Later, I was to read of his degradations and torments – for example, the effect of a diet of skilly upon his digestive system. Now I felt them.

My cell was close to the execution chamber or "the cold meat shed" as it was known. A warder told me, with relish, that it had been used a few hours before I arrived to dispatch a pathetic fellow who had murdered his wife and children. Apparently, his screams had echoed through the prison. Days and then weeks passed in this manner. Did I protest my innocence? Did I demand legal representation? Of course. But apparently spies had no "rights". How long would I remain being held on remand? As long as we "effing" like, I was told.

One morning, about two months later, I lay on my hard bed, watching as a feeble light fanned out from the high, barred window. It consoled me. Light gave life to what it touched. Light was as indomitable as the human spirit. It was love. I cannot describe how exactly but, from that moment, I felt different.

Later that day, I received some unexpected news. I had a visitor. The interview room was dimly lit. At first, I could make out only a silhouette. It was the man's immobility and the rigidity of his posture that gave away his identity. It was my old tormentor, Gribley.

"Good day." His voice showed no emotion. "I trust that you have been keeping well."

"I have stayed in more luxurious accommodation."

"I should imagine so."

He barely looked at me. I was thin and gaunt. My skin was white. He reached down to his jacket pocket, for his pipe. There was a long pause as he filled the bowl with tobacco, compressed it and lit up. I did not say anything. At length, between meditative puffs, he spoke. Gribley astonished me. He offered me a "deal". He said that I could either be convicted as a spy and dangle from the end of a rope, or, enlist in His Majesty's Army for the remainder of the war. After the war, I would be "watched" closely – his reptilian eyes narrowed. Should I accept his proposal and join the army but renege on the bargain and desert, I would be executed immediately, as soon as I was caught.

Gribley said that I could join a regiment of my choice. He seemed to be aware that I had I had been in army cadets at boarding school and so had some knowledge of military matters. It was a chance, he said, to "put something back"; to show that I had some backbone. I merely nodded, looking non-committal. I had entered the room facing death; now the prison door was ajar. He offered me a conciliatory Gold Flake. I took it, eagerly, although I had never been much of a smoker. He watched as I lit up and our smoke commingled. The cigarette was like a glass of warm milk. As I tugged greedily on it, his beady eyes examined my face.

"Very well," I said at last, "I accept."

Gribley asked me whether I would now renounce my treason against the King and "buckle down to it" in the trenches. I assured him that I would. We shook hands. He patted me on the shoulder.

"Good man," he said, "good man."

It had not been a difficult decision. It was better to be a free man in uniform than a prisoner in a condemned cell. And perhaps in the army I would be able to inform someone in a position of influence of the terrible secret that I knew.

Later that day, I was allowed to change back into my civilian clothes. I was given 24 hours in which to settle my affairs, under constant guard. Then I was taken by police car to south London, to begin my new life as a soldier. I don't know why I had chosen the Middlesex Regiment, which was based in Woolwich – they were all the same to me. The regiment is nick-named "The Diehards" because of a heroic incident that occurred during the Peninsular War. I was told about it on my first night in the barracks, by an enthusiastic sergeant major. What could be heroic, I thought, about dying in the name of some bloated Hanoverian king, who could not even speak English?

The barracks were not much more comfortable than Wandsworth Prison, but it was a healthier life. We were up at five o'clock, when it was still dark. The days were filled with ceaseless marching and drill, with rifle shooting and bayonet practice. I learned how to throw a Mills bomb, how to strip down a Lewis gun, and how not to flinch when being screamed at. In order to survive, I quickly acquired a crudeness and blankness of feeling. My instructors said that I was a "natural soldier". I was just the kind of man who was needed in France, especially since the skirmishes in the first months of the war had scythed through officers' ranks. By Christmas, I was on nodding terms with the colonel and was well-versed in the regiment's battle honours. By the following June, I, Austin J. Endicott, the Bloomsbury antiquarian, was a fully-fledged second lieutenant, in charge of four platoons.

The Middlesex Regiment had actually been the first to arrive in France at the onset of the war, in August 1914. I sailed from Dover a year later and joined my company in the village of Vieux Berquin. The regiment, I learned, had just been transferred to the Second Division. On the 19th we marched along dusty white roads to Bethune. Neat green fields stretched to the horizon. The men were still minded to sing jaunty songs. Most of them had yet to see a decomposing body or a human skull poking out of the mud. At the windmill in the village of Hinges, we were inspected by Lord Kitchener himself. He was a small, trim man, almost over-balanced by a huge moustache. He seemed delighted by how neatly we were turned out – that is to say, he nodded.

By nightfall, we had reached our billet at Annequin. The officers were quartered in a rat-infested dug-out that smelt of damp cassocks and mouldy cheese. We were in the Cambrin sector of the front. There were rumours that we would soon be engaged in a titanic battle. It was said that it would involve six divisions, stretching all the way from Loos to the outskirts of Ypres.

Chapter Twelve

Laventie, France
17th of August, 1915

My dear Radu,

*The first thing you should know is this. I am not a brave man.
I am merely in an extraordinary position. I am perhaps only
one of three loyal subjects on the Allied side who knows that
the Germans are developing a new weapon of immense power
with which they hope to win the war. I believe, through certain
documents I have seen, that they have been planning to blow
up the Pyramid of Cheops in Egypt, in order to demonstrate
the weapon's strength. The Allies would be forced to surrender
immediately.*

*Here, close to the front, the air rumbles with explosions;
the night sky flashes with star shells and flares. My battalion,
the 1st of the Middlesex Regiment, will shortly go forward, if
the rumours are true, to engage with the enemy. The great
armies will clash, like the meshing teeth of a huge meat
grinder. It is probable that thousands of men will be killed. I
would like you to tell Ileana, if you are able to speak to her,
that I love her. Please tell here that she is still in my heart and
that I am praying for the day when we shall be together. I only
wish that I had a photograph of her. I hope she will wait for
me.*

*You are Dr. Watson, Radu, to my Sherlock Holmes. I must
therefore tell you what has happened since I left you. I was
apprehended twice by Special Branch. The first time was in
Dover, when I returned there in August, 1914. The second
time, a few weeks later, I was arrested and taken into custody.
I had discovered, through my investigations, the existence of a*

semi-clandestine organisation called the Minerva League. The league has members in many countries up to the highest levels of society, including the Prince of Wales. I believe that it is assisting the Germans in their efforts to develop a "uranium bomb".

In early October, following a burglary that went wrong, I was taken to Bow Street police station in handcuffs. I was charged by the police as a spy. I spent the night in a spartan and freezing cell. The following morning, I was taken to Wandsworth Prison. I was living in fear of death, because spying is a capital offence. An important question now preoccupied me. Why had Special Branch apprehended me and not the members of the Minerva League?

I have formulated three possible explanations:

a) The British authorities are aware of the league's intentions and are observing the situation. I was removed from the scene because I was an impediment to their investigations.

b) The authorities are unaware of the true significance of the Minerva League.

c) Certain influential individuals in the British establishment are "on the side" of the league. In other words, they want the Germans and their allies to win this war.

The third hypothesis is naturally repugnant to me as a patriot. But who knows? We have entered a murky world in which old certainties have been turned upon their head and millions of lives may be casually extinguished on the whim of a few politicians. And is it not conceivable that certain members of the British Royal Family would back the Kaiser?

It is impossible for me to recall Wandsworth Prison without shuddering. It was an environment with horrors I could never have imagined. A few hours previously, I had enjoyed a prosperous and free life, with the respect of my fellows and the liberty of London's streets; now I was like a caged animal, only a few steps from the gallows. After two months, I had an unexpected visitor. It was the Special Branch officer who had arrested me in Highgate. He surprised me. He said that I could either be convicted as a traitor and dangle from a noose, or enlist in His Majesty's Army for the remainder of the war.

I decided that it was better to be dressed in khaki than a woollen prison uniform. At least I would have a fighting chance of surviving and when the war was finished I would be free. Also, as a soldier, I would perhaps be able to act upon my knowledge of the Minerva League. That was the deciding factor. I told the detective that I would accept his offer. The following day, I began my new life. as a recruit of the Duke of Cambridge's own Regiment, the Middlesex, based in Woolwich.

(Letter breaks off here.)

Annequin, France
28th of August, 1915

My Dear Radu,

These lines are snatched in a few precious moments in the battalion dugout. After the mess room in Laventie, it is little more than a cave. It is so close to the front that one can feel the explosions here. The Boche have been strafing us with trench mortars. They know that something is up, but they do not know what it is. Last night, I went out to No-Man's Land with four lads from one of my platoons. This is a fairly quiet part of the line – snipers, rifle grenades and the odd bomb are the main things to worry about. Yesterday, young Davies was killed. The stupid boy was standing on the firing step. A bullet passed clean through his head.

I had thought that soldiering would be an anathema to me

but, do you know, I have been thrown into the society of some of the finest men that I have ever met. Davies is a good example. He was little more than a farm boy. But he had the heart of a lion and that chap would have done anything for you. In one moment, his life was casually extinguished, by a German sniper. After a few days, even his mates will have forgotten about him. They have to. The Grim Reaper is harvesting the souls of thousands of other farm boys from Sussex and Saxony. There is no time to remember them all.

Again, I had thought that the "honour" of the regiment and its roll of honour – Albuhera, Mysore and Waterloo – meant nothing to me. But now, the names make my flesh tingle. I can see how these things happen. Farm boys enlist; they muck in and make the best of it. They are led by idiots – in the army, idiocy is in direct proportion to seniority – but they carry the pride and power of England in their veins. We must be sustained by belief, or our lives are hollow. Who can belittle the integrity of one who is prepared to risk his own life for that of his comrades? Even the discipline of the army has come to seem my friend. My existence was rather lax and structureless before. The army has given me an invaluable gift. I now know how precious life is and that I will never again waste a second of it.

There is a whisper going round that we are going to use poison gas – chlorine – to soften up the German lines in the coming attack. The Boche used it on us six months ago. It is a horror. Who would have thought that human ingenuity could devise such exquisite methods of killing?

This may be my last letter, dear Radu. This Big Push will probably claim just as many lives as the last one. This dugout is a dank and cheerless place. The light here is bad, so it is hard for me to write. I pray that you are safe from harm and ask you, again, to tell Ileana that she is constantly in my thoughts. Tell her that I cannot wait to see her again.

Your affectionate friend

Sherlock Holmes, aka Austin J. Endicott.

My Dear Radu,

What can I say? Except that it is over, and that, thank God, I am still alive. The Germans were laughing as our divisions came at them. They could not believe their luck. The Big Push was a futile and bloody slaughter.

I don't wish to dwell on the details. The most important thing is that I am still in the land of the living. I am in hospital, for the time being. The food is digestible and there is a beautiful horse chestnut tree outside my window. A neat row of them stretches to the road, formerly aligned in the French manner. The battle is over. That is the main thing. I have decided that I will not fight another one. But I had better describe it.

The trenches occupied by the 1st Battalion lay between a railway line and a road. Behind us, was a fortified post called Sims Keep. On our left flank were the Argyll and Sutherland Highlanders; to our right were the Royal Welsh Fusiliers. No-Man's Land in this sector had formerly been grassland. Now, tortured by shells, it was a brown morass. We were to over-run a part of the German line known as "railway trench" and capture a ruined farmhouse just behind it. Our final orders arrived on the 24th of September.

There was heavy rain on the morning of the 25th, which was the day of the attack. My company, D, was in a reserve position. The artillery had been going at the Germans for the past four days. At 5.30am, five thousand cylinders of chlorine were opened up. The gas lay in a thick still cloud over No-Man's Land. There was little wind and what there was blowing the wrong way – back into our lines. The Highlanders got the worst of it. The green gas rolled into their trenches. It must have asphyxiated hundreds of them. I am happy to say that it did not generally prove fatal.

Forty minutes later, our artillery barrage moved back from the German front line. A, B and C companies went over the top. Within a few yards, they were cut to shreds by German machine guns. The Germans must have watched with disbelief. They were standing calmly on their parapet, as their machine guns raked through our lines. Soon, No-Man's Land was filled with dead and dying men.

Before my company moved off we loaded up and fixed bayonets. The lads knew that a hail of lead and almost certain death faced them. The noise was deafening. It was if the enemy were attacking us with a fleet of motorbikes. Just before we went over the top, I looked up. An aeroplane was flying over us. You lucky swine, I thought. I bet you spent last night in a proper bed. That gave me an idea (more of which later). I tried to reassure the men who were closest to me. Their faces had turned grey. Some were praying, others were muttering fearsome oaths.

At 6.50, there was a cacophony of whistles. It was our turn! I heaved myself onto the fire step and over the parapet, waving my revolver. There was still gas about; it burned my eyes and clawed at my throat. Ahead of me were heaps of bodies. Further ahead, were more corpses draped over German barbed wire. No-one had got further than a hundred yards. Bullets were zipping into the mud at my feet. The inevitable happened. One hit me! It felt like a hornet struggling through the folds of my greatcoat. It was not a bad wound. But I did not know it. My left arm flapped uselessly, like a broken wing. I looked back at the trench. Most of the company had not even got out of it. The parapet was covered with bodies, some still twitching.

A dead corporal was lying only yards from my feet. His arms were spread out, as if he had had been crucified. There was only one thing for it – to make for cover or die. Fortunately, providence had placed a shell crater just ahead of me. I rushed forwards as fast as I could, marvelling that I was still alive. My greatcoat felt like lead. I closed my eyes for the last few steps and threw myself forwards. The crater was a quagmire of mud and blood. I lay still. I was shocked to realise that I was not alone; another face was inches from mine. It was a platoon leader from C company, Sergeant Fisk. He was a cockney lad from Bow. We had always got on.

My arm was numb from the shoulder down and blood was trickling down the inside of my sleeve. There was a deafening rush of air. It was a whizz bang. We tensed our bodies but it landed a safe distance away, showering us with fragments. Fisk said that my injury looked like a "Blighty wound". This was what we all wanted – an injury that would get us from away the front but was not serious enough to kill us. Men sometimes attempted to inflict such wounds on themselves. If they were caught at it, they were shot for cowardice.

Poor Fisk's legs had been churned up by bullets. His wounds were infinitely worse than mine. He said that he was one of the only survivors from his platoon, which had gone over in the first wave. There was little that we could do. We were pinned down by a machine gun; to move forwards would have invited certain death. At 1.15 the batallion's survivors were ordered into reserve. But we stayed put. We remained there until after nightfall. I had made tourniquets for Fisk's legs, but he had already lost an enormous amount of blood. I gave him most of the brandy in my hip flask. It seemed to cheer him up a little.

A rescue party got to us just before midnight. There were vivid flashes in the sky from Verey pistols and dazzling balls of red, green and yellow light. Fisk was clinging to life by a thread. His eyes had glazed over. Before the stretcher bearers took him away, I gave his hand a final squeeze and wished him good luck. I had come to an important decision in that crater – that I would escape from this nightmare by any means possible. It was not just to preserve my life. It was my duty to tell someone that there were traitors in the British camp and that the Germans, with their new weapon, may have the ability to break this terrifying war of attrition.

The Germans were holding off from firing as we gathered up our dead. I did not need a stretcher. I stumbled back through our lines, in a daze, clutching my bad arm with my good. The forward trenches were littered with dead bodies and pieces of men and horses. The British commander-in-chief, Sir John French, had directed the battle from a chateau, three miles south of Lillers, using the public telephone system. I wondered whether he would see anything like this. Hundreds of lads, remnants of the Middlesex, the Highlanders and Welsh Fusiliers, all had the same idea. They were making their way to the clearing station.

It was a scene from hell, Radu, almost worse than the battlefield – a livid room, full of the dead and dying, moaning and crying out. After a few hours, a nurse prised a bullet from my arm and gave me a jab for tetanus. A doctor told me that I would not be going back to England. I tried to hide my profound disappointment. He said that I would be sent to a field hospital, near Bethune.

They allowed me out of the hospital today. Bruay-la-Buissiere is a pretty town. I strolled around a church and *lingered in the town square. I examined the church with its mullioned windows and its square Norman tower, thinking of previous wars. I was able to glimpse, for a few hours, what the world would be like if it were at peace.*

I feel that I am blessed, Radu, as I write these lines and the sun pours through my window. I have been saved by some divine intervention. My most important task now is not to be killed. The wound is healing alarmingly quickly. But, if it will not get me back to England, I have other plans.

As always, I send my fondest thoughts to you, and to Ileana. I often dream of Dumbrava de Sus and of the happy times that we spent together in the Pine. I would love to go back there, after this war. It is these thoughts that have kept me going through this hell.

Your good friend

Austin.

Chapter Thirteen

"I should like to fly, sir."

"What?" The colonel looked at me oddly, as if I were about to launch myself from the windowsill.

"I should like to fly".

"I see, Endicott." He frowned.

The colonel had witnessed his share of horrors, but only in the aftermath of each great battle. The trenches had been cleaned up by the time he came to "ginger up" the chaps. His billet in Laventie was as tidy and well-furnished as a Mayfair hotel. He dined regularly and did not see a bloated rat or a severed human limb from one day to the next.

"I should like to be considered for the Royal Flying Corps, sir," I said. "I have submitted an application through Major Greaves and ..."

"Indeed."

"I explained to Major Greaves that I took my ticket at the Cricklewood flying club, before the war," I continued. This was a lie. The ticket was a pilot's licence, issued by the Federation Aeronatique International. It was required of all those who wished to transfer from army regiments into the Royal Flying Corps.

"Unfortunately, the certificate appears to have been lost in the post, sir, as I explained in my application."

I looked into the colonel's face. Did it trouble his conscience that the high-handed incompetence of our commander, French, had just cost the Middlesex Regiment several hundred men in the Loos offensive?

"I see." The colonel did not seem anxious to pursue the matter of the missing document. It was just as well. Cricklewood Flying Club had been a figment of my imagination.

"You realise that you will be reduced to the ranks, at least initially, Endicott." For a moment, his eyes flickered into mine.

"Oh yes, sir. I am quite ready for that." I had rehearsed my next speech. "You see, I have an unusual aptitude for mechanical things. I simply feel that, as a pilot, I will be able to make the best contribution to this war. I do want to do my bit."

"Quite, Endicott."

The colonel did not look convinced. To him, an aeroplane would have seemed more like a toy than a killing machine – a magical contraption conjured from wood, fabric and wire. At any rate, he let me witter on for another minute or so. I had already come out with the same rubbish to Major Greaves.

"I just want to have a crack at the Boche from the air, sir," I concluded.

He did not respond.

"It will be a wrench to leave the regiment. But I have thought about this long and hard, and, in all conscience ..."

"Very well, Endicott."

"I'm sorry?"

He glanced up from the papers on his desk.

"You have my permission. I shall make sure that your request is looked upon favourablt." He paused. "Was there anything else?"

"No, sir." My heart was beating like a row of tappets.

The colonel raised an eyebrow, indicating that the matter was dealt with. He would only have given a little more thought to signing the death warrant of some poor victim of shell-shock.

"Thank you, sir." I was about to lift my arm to salute. The colonel surprised me. He grasped my right hand and stared at me.

His eyes were pale grey. I saw in them the expression of a lost, frightened child.

"Remember, Endicott. You are a Middlesex man and here, where it matters," he touched his chest, "you will always be one. You do know that, don't you?"

"Oh yes, sir."

I felt nauseated. The moist eye-lids, the rigid backbone and the grip, which was a little too firm, combined to evoke a horrible mental picture – that of Brigadier Hinton in his over-heated study in Highgate. I allowed, for I had little choice, his hand to linger on mine. It tingled as if the colonel were connected to an electric current. I had had a bellyful of men like him. I had vowed to put the stupid war behind me and this idiot, with his watery eyes and his clammy hands, was giving me the means to do so.

"Thank you, oh thank you, sir" I said, trying to look sincere.

Can you imagine how refreshing it was to live in a tidy hut, to sleep in clean pygamas and to eat decent grub, with proper cutlery, served on a tablecloth? After the squalor of my billet at Annequin, the School of Military Aeronautics at St. Omer was like heaven. The flyers' war was a clean war. Pilots looked down on the men sprawling in the mud of the trenches with pity; you poor devils, they thought. Infantry men glanced up at pilots feeling a similar emotion. To them, aviators were ludicrously exposed.

The routines of the school were well-established. Up at six, breakfast and then a parade. We then broke into squadrons of ten, to go into the classroom. We had no marks of rank, but wore a white band around our peaked caps. The dress code was relaxed. Breeches and puttees were supposed to be worn; in practice, the code was rarely enforced. Oddly, the only real rule was that we were to wear our Sam Browne belts at all times.

The casual attitude that prevailed in the RFC appealed to

me, compared to the mindless rigidities of the army. Many of the chaps failed to turn up to lessons; some even missed Monday morning parades. But I enjoyed the classroom sessions and was an attentive student. I did not want to get killed because I had been looking out of the window.

I was extremely lucky to learn to fly in an Avro 504. They were not particularly fast (the top speed was 82 mph) but they were far lighter and more manoeuvrable than the old BE2cs. Perhaps it is not really surprising that I took to flying so well. I like machines; even their smell makes my heart quicken. I have good reflexes and I am blessed with keen eyesight.

On my second day of tuition, the first under dual instruction, the instructor, MacLeish, asked me whether I was good at cricket. I nodded, a sick feeling rising in my gorge. "Then you'll make a good pilot, laddy," he assured me. It was a cloudy morning. The other cadets watched us, nervously, from the side of the field. Most days, at least one cadet was killed or seriously injured and ambulances and fire tenders were on constant stand-by.

I climbed into the front seat of the cockpit. MacLeish told me to rest my hands and feet lightly on the controls. I was to "feel" their response as he piloted the machine. A fitter turned over the variable pitch propeller. Our ears were assailed by a noisy clatter; it was hard to hear his words through the speaking tube. MacLeish made a signal with his hand. Chocks away! He steered the Avro into the wind. Slowly, we picked up speed.

I had only joined the RFC as a means of escape. I had not reckoned on the sheer thrill of flying; of the joy of feeling one's stomach lurch into one's mouth and of being deafened and battered by the wind and engulfed in hot fumes. I knew that morning that I would only be content once I had mastered this art, adding to flying, which was hard enough, the complexities of maps, machine guns and cameras. It would not be easy. Accomplishing everything at the same time would be rather like playing noughts and crosses with one hand, while spinning a plate on a stick with the other.

That morning, I completed little more than a succession of take-offs and landings. The Avro had a pair of skids beneath the nose, so that you could tip it forwards without suffering a catastrophe. MacLeish also showed me how to flow from rudder to aileron when taxiing, to prevent sliding. He did not swear at me, or hit me on the back of the head with a spanner. These were good signs. Most cadets went solo only after a couple of hours on dual control, but it was clear that I would be ready a lot sooner.

After our final landing, he offered neither praise nor discouragement. He merely told me not to be so damn eager. A good pilot, he said, only had one characteristic. He was still alive. MacLeish, who had recently survived an almost fatal crash, was a careful and thorough man. The difference between life or death, he told me, could lie in the cleanness of one's goggles. He said that one should study the psychology and habits of the enemy and, ideally, only engage with him when one knew that one had the advantage.

I did not fly solo until the following week. It was a grey day and the sky was oozing with moisture. MacLeish was watching. If I was going to be killed, it was most likely to be now. The smell of the wet grass reminded me of going out to bat at boarding school. I felt the same sense of dread mixed with excitement; the same desire not to let the side down. However, as soon as the plane moved off, I relaxed. I knew, somehow, that everything would be all right.

MacLeish had told me to stay well beneath the clouds. I was simply to circle the airfield twice and come down in one piece. I lifted off smoothly and accomplished a graceful climbing turn. I felt a sense of delight as the Avro responded to the controls. I cannot explain why; using the joy stick and rudder always seemed "natural" to me. I enjoyed looking down at the huts, like little toys, and the white confetti of the cadets' upturned faces. I relished banking a little too steeply on my second circuit and waggling my wings, directly over the cadets. Twenty minutes later, I achieved a neat three-point landing, taxied to the edge of the field and came to a perfect stop. Later, in private, MacLeish called me an idiot for showing off. But he did not upbraid me in front of the other cadets. He merely smiled and patted me on the shoulder.

After my first solo effort, came more ambitious flights. Once I breasted the clouds and climbed to 9,000 feet. Up there, the air was so icy and thin up that it scarcely seemed to hold one up. I now thought of little else but flying. Early mornings were the best time, as the sun was breaking through the belt of trees at the edge of the airfield. In my flying helmet and fleece-lined jacket, I felt like Odysseus; the sky was my wine dark sea.

Death was commonplace at St. Omer. At the end of some days, the edge of the field was littered with charred, twisted wreckages. We tried to be light-hearted each time a cadet did not return to take his place at dinner, but, really, we were not. I loved flying and I felt as one with the other men in the mess. But there was an important difference between them and me. I had no intention of engaging with the enemy as a pilot. My goal was to escape to England. And I would do so as soon as the best opportunity presented itself.

One morning in late November, MacLeish took me on a cross-country trip to take a peek at the front line. Far beneath us, the Yser Canal twisted like a snake towards the dark stain of Ypres. I was sitting in the back of the cockpit, attempting to match what I saw on the map with the blurred smudges below. The trenches of both armies traversed shattered woods and plains of mud. In the distance, one could see villages and the square towers of churches. We tried to stay on our own side of the front. To the south of the Ypres salient were some allied kite balloons, moored by steel cables. We got close enough to wave to their occupants. I could only feel sorry for those chaps; they were human versions of tin ducks at a fairground.

It had been MacLeish's intention to show me what anti-aircraft fire, known as "archie" looked and felt like. East of Ypres, he got his wish when an anti-aircraft battery opened up. MacLeish pulled back the stick as high explosive rent the air, buffeting our fragile machine. I knew that I would never forget the smell of the bursting shells. From above, they seemed to dissolve like puff-balls in a shower of white dust. It was like being in the middle of a firework display. MacLeish twisted in his seat and looked back. The aircraft was bucking like a horse. He was grinning. I felt sick to my stomach. I must have looked as pale as a glass of milk.

However, worse was to come. After turning in a wide circle, MacLeish suddenly thrust the stick forward and we began to dive. The wind roared through the biplane's wings, turning our fragile craft into a howling banshee. At one point, the air-speed must have been nudging 200. I gripped my stick for dear life, thinking that the wings would be torn off.

"Dear God," I thought, "he is going to bomb the anti-aircraft battery."

It was true. At 5,000 feet the archie started to burst around us again. At that point we were pointing virtually straight down. I was pinned to my seat as if a ten-ton weight were pushing on my chest. I thought that my ear-drums would burst. We were almost over the target when MacLeish released the bomb. There was a shudder through the fuselage as the little plane shed its heavy load. At last, he pulled out of the dive and we began to climb. I felt a huge sense of relief. We had heard the bomb detonate, but we did not see if it had done any good. Probably, it had just concussed a few earthworms.

However, we were not troubled by archie again, as we made our way back to the allied lines.

Chapter Fourteen

The RE7 (standing for Reconnaissance Experimental No. 7) was a pig to fly. This was because its top speed, of around 70 miles per hour, was not much faster than the speed at which it stalled. The aeroplane had been designed to carry a range of equipment – two Lewis guns, a Vickers gun, cameras and a 500lb bomb. The result was that the wretched machine could barely get off the ground. It was impossible to be delicate with the controls. One had to wrench the joystick and the rudder, hoping, or indeed praying, that the aircraft would follow. It was a death-trap.

In January, having won my wings, I was stationed with 21 Squadron. Equipped solely with RE7s, it had just transferred to France. No. 21 was based at Boisdinghem airfield, close to St. Omer. It was a reconnaissance unit. Its main tasks were to find targets, guide artillery fire and take photographs. But the RE7 was so vulnerable to attack that it could not fly un-escorted. Typically, four RE7s would take to the air, accompanied by BE2Cs, FE8s and a Bristol Fighter – up to twelve aircraft. Later, No. 21 came to be known as the "suicide squadron". I was indeed fortunate that I was only with it for two weeks.

Leaving the airfield was a wrench. I had spent a pleasant Christmas at Boisdinghem, toasting the king with plum brandy. One morning, I forced myself out of bed before dawn. I was not wearing my normal flying clothes but instead a thick black jacket over many layers of clothing. I had smeared my face with Vaseline. It was a good protection against the cold. I had told a fitter, the night before, that I wanted to become more familiar with the RE7's controls. He was waiting for me in the hanger. He raised an eyebrow when he saw that I was carrying a canvass kit-bag. However, he did not say anything. I needed a mechanic to turn the prop of the aircraft, to allow me to take off.

Within an hour, I was flying over the English Channel. It was just after dawn and not many English people were awake, I had crossed the chalk cliffs of Kent. I had no desire to run into an anti-Zeppelin patrol. I made my way down the coast, looking for a likely field. There wasn't one. The coast road looked safer, so I brought the aircraft down on it, close to the village of Dymchurch. I did not wish to stay with the aircraft for too long. I switched off the engine, jumped down from the cockpit and ran for the nearest hedge.

East Kent is a bleak place in winter. A light rain was falling, which would not let up for the entire day. Ahead of me, grey, flat and uninviting, stretched the Romney Marsh. I was cold but I was not depressed. I was determined that the next few weeks would resolve the question of the Minerva League once and for all. They may end up with me being arrested and hanged, but at least I would have done my best.

I set off across a wet field, impelled by a distant yet achievable goal. It took me four days to reach London! You will probably think that I was mad and that I should merely have hopped onto a train. Remember the situation I was in. As soon as the RFC had realised that I was absent without leave, they would inform Special Branch and then every police constable from Herne Bay to Hendon would be on the look out for pilot officer Endicott.

I carried in my kit-bag my army groundsheet to sleep in, an oilskin coat, a shaving kit, soap, a water-bottle and some spare clothes. Tucked into the groundsheet were my Webley revolver and 12 rounds of ammunition – just in case. I also had a formidable dagger with a serrated blade (a souvenir of the trenches) and some English money. To fortify the inner man, I had stolen some butter and bread rolls from the cookhouse.

At the end of the first day, hideously wet, hungry and cold, I reached the Kent village of Hartley, in the Weald. I spent the night in a forest, wedged beneath a wall. The second day was even more uncomfortable. By the time I had reached Tunbridge Wells my feet were blistered and I was ravenous. I slept, nervously, in an outbuilding. The following morning, I abandoned my original plan of walking. With trepidation, I boarded a motorbus bound for Woolwich, wrapped up in my coat. From there, I hopped onto an over-burdened electric tram. This took me all the way to the Victoria Embankment.

Central London was a far more grim and bad tempered place than when I had left it more than a year before. A partial black-out was being observed. Many shops and all of the city's museums had been closed. People looked at one warily. Thoughtfully, I walked along Northumberland Avenue, towards Trafalgar Square. It had stopped raining, but my clothes were sodden and my feet protested at each step.

A homing instinct or perhaps morbid curiosity was guiding me towards the Exhibition Rooms. It would not be safe for me to enter them. I planned to linger outside, to spy the lie of the land and then to find a lodging house; the following day, I would visit Harry Hawkins' mother in Hampstead. I wished to find out if Harry had done anything to inform the world about the Minerva League. Then I could work out my next move.

Slowly, I made my way along Haymarket onto Shaftesbury Avenue. I made a forlorn figure, trudging in front of barely-illuminated theatres which were gamely playing musical comedies. Disguised in my raincoat and flatcap, I felt furtive and vaguely disreputable. I did not wish anyone to inquire too closely who I was and there was a remote possibility, especially as I approached Soho, that somebody might recognise me. I crossed High Holborn. It was now quite dark but the theatre and pub crowds were not yet out; the streets were strangely quiet. I passed the Prince's Theatre, which had always been one of my favourites.

The theatre was playing a comic opera – *The Boatswain's Mate* by Ethel Smyth. I was now assisted by an amazing coincidence. The musical play interested me and I happened to glance at the list of players, which was pasted onto a board by the entrance. Immediately, a name that I recognised jumped out at me. It was that of Katie Kidd, a close friend of Harry Hawkins! I recalled the gay nights that we had spent together in 1914. The war had not been such a horror then – there was an innocence in the enthusiasm of the populace towards "our boys". Seeing her name now was a rare stroke of luck. For Katie would undoubtedly know where Harry was. Perhaps she could arrange a meeting.

A simple plan presented itself. *The Boatswain's Mate* was being performed that night. I had merely to pass a couple of hours in a public house and then to intercept Katie at the stage door, as she was leaving the theatre.

Katie had not changed at all. She was petite and vivacious with auburn ringleted hair, cut short, and a gap-toothed smile. She was wearing a tailored blue jacket, a pleated skirt of the same colour and a high-necked white blouse.

At first, my presence caused astonishment and then undisguised delight.

"Austin!"

She grasped my hand.

"I can't believe it! Is it you?"

"Of course it is me."

"Where have you been?"

I shrugged.

"You are looking ..."

She did not finish the sentence. The adjectives cold, wet and half-starved would probably have fitted the bill.

"It is so good to see you Austin. Come." She pulled me into the doorway and kissed me on the cheek.

I was somewhat startled. Turning around, I noticed that a peculiar apparition was approaching the stage door. The figure was dressed in a tweed suit, with gleaming white spats. It wore a felt hat, from which a feather jutted jauntily.

"Ethel," said Katie. "I am busy at the moment. This is my good friend, Austin."

The figure eyed me beadily and took a puff from a cigar.

"If you will excuse us ..."

"I see."

The figure blew out a cloud of smoke in a gesture of resignation. Then it turned and disappeared into the night.

"Who was that?" I said.

"That was Ethel Smyth. She is the author of the play I am in, *The Boatswain's Mate*."

"That was a woman?" I said. "I thought it was a ..."

"I know." Katie smiled. "She is a famous suffragette, as well as being a composer and playwright. She wrote the suffragettes' anthem, you know, *The March of the Women*. She has been hounding me for weeks. I am so glad that you are here, Austin. You have rescued me."

"And saved your virtue?"

"Probably."

Katie giggled. I blushed, regretting my remark.

"Now, Austin," she said, composing herself. "You are looking terrible. What are we going to do with you? Do you have anywhere to stay tonight?"

I shook my head.

"Then you must come with me."

She smiled sweetly.

"That is most kind of you," I said, "you see, I cannot go back to my house in Highbury, because ..."

She silenced me. With a female's infallible instinct, she had grasped the situation.

"I understand, Austin."

"Where do you live?"

"Very close to here. Come."

She took my hand and led me from the theatre. It had started to rain again. Soon, we were making our way down Drury Lane, stepping over puddles and sheltering beneath her umbrella.

Katie's career had gone from strength to strength since I had last met her. After featuring in several reviews, one before the king, she had appeared in a "hit", a play called *Push and Go* at the Hippodrome, starring the celebrated American actress, Shirley Kellogg. Music was her forte. She had a strong soprano voice, which soared above the chorus. She was required to sing solo in *The Boatswain's Mate*, which was supposed to be a comedy, and also to speak a few lines.

Her rooms were in King Street, overlooking the Royal Opera House. There were two of them – a living room with a divan bed and, through an arch, a small kitchen. It was the abode of an actress, softly-lit and decorated with peacock feathers, oriental vases and playbills.

She placed her hands on her hips and appraised me.

"Austin, you must get out of those clothes. You are soaking."

However hard she tried, Katie could not disguise Yorkshire from her voice. She was from Huddersfield.

"I am sorry," I said.

She looked at me mischievously.

"Don't worry, I shan't molest you. Are those the only clothes you have?"

I nodded.

"Tomorrow, I shall sort you out."

I looked around the small room. Where could I take off my trousers?

Katie had anticipated my question. She pulled out a screen,

decorated with Chinese designs, and unfolded it in a corner of the room. But what was I to wear? She handed me a voluminous, burgundy-coloured dressing gown.

"It is Harry's," she explained, "sometimes he ..."

"Stays here?"

Now it was her turn to be embarrassed. I have never seen a face turn so red.

"I am sure that it will fit you, Austin" she said. "You and Harry are about the same size."

Her voice cracked.

"What's wrong?"

"It's Harry. I don't know if he is ..."

She began to sob. Without meaning to, I took her in my arms. Her small, frail body was trembling. It convulsed with each intake of breath.

"Never mind," I said. "I know Harry. I know some of the scrapes he has been in. Please don't worry."

Katie nestled into my body. She cried out in broken gasps. Presently, she began to murmur. I stroked her hair, moist from the rain, feeling the rise and fall of her chest.

"Where do you think Harry is?"

We were sitting in the kitchen, the following morning. Coffee had never tasted better. I had spent an uncomfortable night, sleeping on a thin quilt on the floor, but my body was reviving with each intake of the sweet liquid.

Katie looked tired. She wore a white straight dress.

"He is on an island in the Aegean. At least I hope he is."

"How is that?"

"Didn't he tell you that he had joined the army?"

"No. I have been in France, as I told you. I have not heard from Harry for more than a year. I did write to him."

She looked at me.

"He joined the Hampshire Regiment, last Christmas. They

made him a second lieutenant. In March, he sailed for Gallipoli."

"Gallipoli?"

"I received a letter from Valletta, in Malta. They stopped there on the way. He said that he was playing billiards."

"That's just like Harry," I said. "I bet there was money at stake."

"They landed at a place called Cape Helles – cape hell, Harry called it."

"Was there fighting?"

"I think so. It is hard to tell from the letter, a lot of it had been blanked out. The Hampshire Regiment were with the Norfolks. I think that they tried to fight their way onto the peninsula. But the Turks stopped them and they dug in. Harry said that the flies and the heat were terrible. He caught dysentery. That is why he missed the next big attack."

"That was lucky."

She looked doubtful.

"In August there was another battle. He was wounded in the chest with shrapnel."

"Has he been evacuated from Gallipoli?"

"Yes."

Her face looked haunted.

"His last letter was from a hospital on the island of Lemnos. He was very ill. He said that they had made him a captain."

"Captain Hawkins." I said, softly.

"It sounds strange doesn't it? His mother is very proud of him. If, I mean when he comes back, we are going to ..."

Involuntarily, she touched her finger – the one where her engagement ring should be.

"Get married?"

"Yes. He asked me in his letter."

"Have you replied?"

"Of course."

"And?"

"I have heard nothing. I am still waiting."

She sighed. I feared that she would cry again.

"Listen," I said. "I know Harry. He is the world's worst correspondent, which is peculiar, considering his profession. Do you know, when we were at prep school, he was the only boy who didn't write to his mother. That's terrible, isn't it?"

"Do you think that he is ..."

"Alive? Of course he is. A bit of shrapnel. That's not going to kill Harry."

Her eyes were still wet.

Austin," she said. "I am so glad that you came to the theatre. Do you believe in fate? I do. I knew that you would come. Look."

She stood up.

"There is something that I must show you. Before Harry left for Gallipoli, he gave me something."

She crossed to a small bureau at the side of the room and unlocked it. Inside, was a leather bag. She handed it to me.

"I have had it all this time. But I didn't know what to do with it."

She watched, intently, as I opened it.

"Harry," I murmured to myself, as I surveyed the contents. "You absolute bloody genius."

Chapter Fifteen

There was a letter in the bag. I read it first. It was sealed in a
lined envelope, addressed to me. The letter was written
hurriedly in pencil. Harry's handwriting had always been
terrible. It was dated the 15th of March, 1915.

Dear Austin,

*Greetings, old friend. It is good to talk. You will no doubt be
relieved to see these lines. First, you will be astounded to
learn that I have joined up! I hitched my wagon to the Royal
Hampshires at a recruiting station in Fulham. As you know, I
love sailing and coast of Hampshire has always been dear to
me. Why did I take the king's shilling? Primarily, because I
was tired of people staring and pointing at me in the street.
Cowardly, I know.*

*The bad, or perhaps good, thing is that that they are
sending my battalion overseas. Not to France, because we are
sailing from Avonmouth. My guess is (don't tell anybody) that
we are heading for the Dardanelles, to have a crack at Johnny
Turk. I am on a two-day pass before embarkation and tonight
will be my last one with Katie. I am writing this, Austin,
because I owe you an explanation – I owe you many
explanations for my failings and derelictions. I shall give the
letter to Katie, to give to you.*

*Regarding that night in Belgravia. I am truly sorry that I
left you to face the consequences of something that was my
idea. Once again, I have got you into the most fearful trouble,
just like when we were at school. You will no doubt want to
know what happened. Well, when I heard a commotion in the
hallway, I went out through the study window, into the teeth of
a frightful storm. I had had a good look at the building on the
way in and I knew that there was a ledge just beneath. The*

trouble was, it was little more than six inches wide! I felt my way along it, buffeted by the wind and the rain and absolutely terrified. I came to the window of another apartment. It was dark. I prayed that there was no-one inside. It was a sash window and had not been locked. I managed to lift the lower pane and climb inside. I laid low until the police had gone. Then I let myself out. It was easy.

I knew that you had been arrested. Naturally, I thought about you and I tried to find out where the police had taken you. I made some inquiries through third parties, including Katie, but I could not establish where you were. As far as the police were concerned, there had been no break-in on that night in Belgravia. And as far as the world was concerned, Austin J. Endicott had simply disappeared.

From Sir James Folie's study, I obtained several more documents (see enclosed) further incriminating the Minerva League. When I told my editor, Morris, at the Evening News *about what we had stumbled across, he merely laughed. He did not stop laughing for five minutes. He said that the* News *was not in the business of publishing imaginative fiction – perhaps I should try* The Strand Magazine. *He has always been an ass. This left me with a dilemma. What could I do? To whom could I show the documents? I knew that if I went to the police, I should suffer the same fate as you and be arrested.*

You will probably think that it was wrong of me to run away from the problem by joining the Hampshires. But that is the decision I made, and I must live with it. This thing may be too big for us, Austin. We are only mortals. I do not think that you realise the strength of the forces that we are up against. At any rate, I hope that the papers that I have left with Katie will help you to ensure that the guilty men are collared. It's a good job that you have the soul of a bulldog.

I do not know if you will ever read this letter. As for my own life, it is now in the hands of others. In some ways, it is a relief to be denied the burden of free will. I pray that you are safe, and that, one day, you will find it in your heart to forgive me. It is over to you now. Good luck in whatever you do.

affectionate regards

Harry.

PS Please keep Katie safe for me. She is very precious.

"What does it say, Austin?"
"You can read it."
"Are you sure?"
"Of course."
I handed the paper to Katie, then I examined the contents of the leather bag. Inside, were the membership records of the Minerva League. The names listed included some exremely high-ranking and influential people. One name in particular surprised me, that of ——————— . *(Editor's note: several words have been blanked out in the manuscript.)* This document must have been among those stolen by Sammy the Shim from Minerva House in November 1914. I found the letter from Brigadier Hinton to Sir James Folie that Harry had shown me that night in my club and copies of other letters, some referring to Operation Siegfried. There was also a large map or plan. I unfolded it.

"What is it, Harry?"
"It appears to be a diagram of one of the pyramids. Take a look."
Katie crossed to my side of the table. She had just washed her hair. She smelled of soapsuds and lily of the valley. She bent her head close to mine.
The drawing represented the interior of the Great Pyramid of Cheops, or Khufu. It was dated November the 12th, 1913.

A complicated network of passages and shafts was shown. One of the interior structures, at the top of an ascending passage was labeled the King's Chamber. The King's Chamber was marked with an X. Notes had been made at the sides of the drawing in tiny but meticulous handwriting. I assumed that this was the autograph of Sir James Folie. The notes described in detail how several tons of refined hedonite could be embarked across the desert from the Nile, transported to the great monumental structure and placed at the heart of the pyramid.

"So, it is true then," I said.

"What is true?"

"This is the proof." I jabbed the diagram with my finger. "The Minerva League is planning to blow up the Great Pyramid!"

"Are they?"

Katie looked unimpressed.

"Did you find the piece of rock?"

"The what?"

"Look in the bottom of the bag, Austin."

I rummaged there as she had directed. My fingers closed around a small, hard object. I pulled out a dark-coloured pebble flicked with red.

"Good heavens," I said. "It's the Blood Stone!"

I placed it the palm of my hand and tested its weight. I felt ridiculously pleased.

"Do you know what this is, Katie?"

"I have no idea."

"It is a piece of hedonite. My father used to keep it on display in his shop."

"Was it stolen, then?" Her eyes widened.

"Yes. Two years ago. Did Harry not tell you?"

"No."

The stone, which had been removed from my safe in the

Exhibition Rooms, must have either been taken by Sammy the Shim from Minerva House or by Harry from Sir James Folie's study. I knew that my safe had been cracked by someone acting for Special Branch. How on earth had the Blood Stone got into the hands of the Minerva League? For the moment, I had no answer.

"I am delighted to see this again," I said.

"I am glad, Austin. You will be able to touch it, when you need good luck."

She smiled, showing the adorable gap between her front teeth.

"We could certainly do with some."

I slipped the mineral into my trouser pocket. It nestled comfortably there.

"Are you hungry, Katie?"

"A little, yes."

"Is that Lyons corner house still there? The one in Coventry Street?"

"I think so."

"Do you know, I used to think about it when I was living on bully beef. It would be marvellous to have some supper there."

She frowned.

"I shall go with you on one condition."

"And what is that?"

"That you wear some new clothes. I shall find some for you. It will be a tonic for you, Austin."

She smiled like an angel.

"Of course," I said, feeling doubtful.

That afternoon, I rested on Katie's bed. I was dog-tired and I slept like a baby, undisturbed by the nightmares that had been troubling me of late. Katie woke me in the afternoon, saying, ominously, that she would like to "dress" me. I was not really in the mood. But I went along with it.

She had borrowed the clothes from the wardrobe master at the Prince's Theatre. The suit was cut from a herringbone tweed. It was not my kind of thing at all. There was a crisp white shirt, with a new collar and cuffs, and a scarlet tie. Katie had also obtained a pair of brogues, a new fedora and a camel-hair overcoat.

I felt self-conscious stepping from behind the screen.

"What's wrong?"

"Nothing," I said. I felt like Ethel Smyth – a man dressed up as a woman pretending to be a man.

"It's just that ..."

"You look very handsome. See for yourself."

She pointed to her dressing mirror.

"Are you sure?"

"Of course I am."

I appraised my reflection. My face seemed awfully pale, my cheeks were hollow. The jacket felt tight around my shoulders.

"I am not carrying the cane," I said.

"I shall not force you."

The shadow of a smile flickered across my face.

"That's better, Austin. I shall feel proud walking besides you."

"Really?"

"Of course."

She took my arm.

"Let's go for dinner."

It had been an uncomfortable meal. Throughout it, I had felt people's eyes boring into my back. In these clothes, I was far too conspicuous. How long would it be before there was tap on my shoulder and someone started asking uncomfortable questions?

I had brought my revolver with me, loaded with a full

cylinder, much to Katie's amusement. It nestled in a leather holster against my breast-bone. It was not that I wanted to kill anyone – even in the war, I had never knowingly done so – merely that I could not afford to be captured. If I were, the game would be up.

Close to Piccadilly Circus, this corner house had once been a terminus of liveliness and gaiety. Now, it had an air of mournful abandonment. Two of its floors had been closed off. Only disgruntled old ladies seemed to eat here and wary men in uniform. Even the waitresses, once famed for their vivacity, were tired and careworn.

"Austin?"

"You don't have to eat it."

"I know."

I prodded my chop experimentally. It was as dry and tough as a boot sole.

"I used to come here a lot," I said.

"Really?"

"Before the war. Did you ever see *Pygmalion*, Katie? Beerbohm Tree was in it, at His Majesty's Theatre in the Haymarket. The last time I was here ..."

"Austin."

Her firm look stopped me in my tracks.

"Someone is staring at us."

Here we go, I thought.

"What does he look like?"

"He is a soldier. A corporal. He is wearing a cap and a ..."

"What colour is his cap, Katie?"

"Red."

My heart sank. It was just my luck that a military policeman had wandered in.

"What is he doing?"

"He is hovering in the doorway."

"Give me your keys," I said, "quickly. But don't let him

see."

Katie fumbled in her bag. She slid the keys across the table, in her fist.

"I am going to leave," I said. "Sorry, but there is no alternative. I shall pretend that I am going to the er ..."

"When will I see you?"

"I don't know, Katie."

Panic came into her eyes.

"I'll go back to your rooms, to change out of these clothes," I said. "Then I must go into hiding. But I shall make contact with you, I promise. You must stay terrifically calm. If you can, try to hold the fellow up. He is sure to come over in a minute or two. Can you do that?"

She nodded.

"Katie ..."

I stood up and leaned forwards. I placed a hand on her shoulder and kissed her on the nape of the neck, as if we were lovers. With my other hand, I took the keys from her moist grip. I gave her hand a squeeze. It was lucky that I knew the layout of this restaurant. A passage in front of me led to the cloakrooms. At the end of it was the kitchen. My escape route. As I stood up, I glanced over my shoulder.

I saw him then – a short, thickset man with a blue chin. Military policemen were an unpopular breed. During battles, they would wait behind the front lines to sift out the genuinely wounded from "stragglers", traumatised men who were drifting back to safety from forward positions. They would bully and prod these unfortunates back to their units, sarcastically threatening death by firing squad for those who did not comply. Most of us hated MPs. They were generally known as "cherry knobs".

Oh Lord. He was coming towards me.

"Sir, may I see your ..."

Heels, I thought. I ran for it. At the end of the corridor was

145

a door with a frosted glass panel. With the Red Cap only a few paces behind, I barged through. An ancient man in stained chef's whites stared at me, frozen. He was opening his mouth as my pursuer crashed into the room. In readiness, I had drawn my weapon.

"Stop!"

The Red Cap's momentum caused him to stumble forwards. Steadying my right arm with my left, I trained my gun on his fat head. We looked into each other's eyes. His were dark, beneath a simian brow. His hand was hovering over his holster.

"If you stay perfectly still, nothing will happen to you."

He guffawed.

"And if I don't?"

I did not flinch. My arm was like a girder. My Webley Mark 6 revolver was the latest 1915 issue. It was a lovely thing, with a six-inch barrel and a removable front sight. I had kept it dry and well-oiled. It was a double-action weapon. That meant that only one pull of the trigger would blow the Red Cap's head off. He knew that.

"That's for you to find out, isn't it?"

"I don't think you have the nerve."

His face betrayed no emotion. He would have made a good bridge player, if he had had the brains, which he almost certainly didn't.

"The nerve for what?"

"To kill me."

I made no reply.

"Kill him then," he said.

"What?"

The poor chef was had shrunk with fear. His face was like chalk. This was a direct provocation. How could I ignore it? In most confrontations there is a moment that settles who will win. I sensed that this was it. Close to the Red Cap's stomach, was a pan of hot oil, bubbling over a fierce flame. The chef was glancing at it nervously.

I have always been a good shot; I was by the far the best in the army cadets and, at Woolwich, I almost invariably won the marksman's jackpot – a cup of sixpences – on the firing range. There is a knack to it. It it simply a question of emptying one's mind and controlling one's breathing.

I lowered the barrel of my gun and squeezed the trigger. The revolver jumped back. The frying pan exploded like a phosphorous bomb, showering boiling oil onto its hapless victim. The Red Cap's shrill scream filled the restaurant. I hoped that his tunic had caught the brunt of the hot oil, not his face. However, I was not going to stay to find out.

One thing was bothering me. Military policemen normally hunted in packs – usually, there were at least two of them. Perhaps there would be a second one skulking by the back door. There was an icy clarity in the spaces between the seconds. The chef had wrapped his head in his arms. He was whimpering with fear. Surprise would be my best tactic. I simply kicked at the street door, like a bolting horse. It yielded. There was no-one outside. Only a rancid courtyard, redolent of overflowing dustbins.

It was raining quite heavily. The light camelhair coat would keep me dry. But I would ditch it for my oilskin as soon as I reached Katie's. I had learnt a lesson that evening – to move back from the footlights and meld into the shadows. Fortunately, I knew these streets intimately; they had protected, nurtured and offered me entertainment for more than two decades. And I could glide through them as easily as a poacher at night on a country estate.

Within ten minutes, I had arrived at King Street. I did not linger there. I simply changed into my anonymous clothes and placed the things that I needed into my kit-bag. I rolled up the letters and papers that Harry had given to Katie into the plan of pyramid and crammed this into the bag too. The Blood Stone, my faithful old friend, I placed in my jacket pocket. I positioned Katie's keys on the mantelpiece and slipped out of her rooms like a ghost, leaving the door slightly ajar, so that she could get in.

Where, in the name of Lucifer, was I to go? The problem was, I did not know Harry's mother well enough to ask her to put me up. As fresh air hit my face, I had had an inspiration – Sammy the Shim's lodging house in Whitechapel! If he was not fertilising the Flanders mud, which was quite possible, the rogue could fill me in on his exploits. Sammy, if anyone, would know how to lie low in London as a deserter. Perhaps he had heard from Harry.

My dark coat felt like a cloak of invisibility. Wondering what the Red Cap was doing now, I walked to Theobald's Road and took an electric tram through Clerkenwell. Despite the time of night, it was crammed with ill-tempered passengers. There were few cars on the roads, because of petrol rationing. That meant that the trams and taxis were always full. And you can forget any notion that people were nice to each other. It was every person for themself – large or small, male or female. I jumped off at Old Street. On foot, I now crossed the invisible boundary that marked the East End, with its gaudy gin palaces, raucous music halls and infamous public houses, from the rest of London.

It was far too late to be doing this. Feeling nervous, I rapped on the blistered front door of Sammy's place, in Fournier Street. Amazingly, the landlady was the same crone who Harry and I had knocked up in 1914. And she was in the same foul mood.

"Yes," she hissed through brown teeth.

I did not have time to reply.

"You want lodgings, I suppose."

It was a rebuke rather than an offer.

"It's five shillings. You must pay me for the week and I shall have the money now."

Five shillings! Inflation had certainly taken hold of London. As I fumbled in my pocket, she placed a fat hand on her hip.

"I see. Could I possibly ..."

"You shall not see the room first. You 'as already ruined my sleep. It is only my generosity what has kept you orf the streets."

The matron reached beneath her sagging bosoms to pocket the coins.

"Come wiv me."

Clutching a formidable set of keys, she led me down a dark hallway smelling of coal gas. A dully glowing mantle beckoned us up the creaking stairs. We reached the landing and a familiar door. There was one problem. This had been Sammy's room, so clearly he could not be here. The landlady slid one of her keys into a hole. Her wrinkled yellow face leered into mine.

"We is 'ere. You must fetch for yourself now."

Before I could say thank you, she had turned away and was waddling down the stairs.

One step down, she looked back.

"Is you a soldier?"

"Yes," I said, unconvincingly. "I am on leave."

My lie had not convinced her for one second.

"I will ask no questions. But you must ask me none neither. Is that understood? It is your conscience and you must live with it."

"Of course."

She sniffed and continued her downward progress.

Chapter Sixteen

How can I describe the smell? It was light and floral, but also heavy, and sickly, almost beyond endurance There were other notes in it too, Macassar oil and juniper, or possibly sandalwood. I did not identify its main element from my own experience; rather from my friend Harry's descriptions of his expeditions down to Limehouse for the *Evening News*. It was opium!

The room was dark, except for the light of a small candle which was placed in the centre of a low table. Within its aura, I could make out a man, sitting in a well-padded armchair. His hands rested comfortably upon his abdomen. Straggly black hair framed his sallow, angular face. He was looking down. In the poor light, I could not see his eyes. One could sense from his composure that he had been sitting in this posture for a long time. Perhaps hours. Next to the candle, was a small silver pipe and an ashtray. I wondered how the man's smoking habits had not been detected by the harridan who presided over this miserable house.

I edged forwards, with the utmost trepidation.

"Come in, my friend. Don't be shy."

"Is Sammy ..."

"Sammy has gone."

"Where?"

"It does not matter. I have been waiting."

"For me?"

"Perhaps. I knew that the bearer of the task would have a corporeal form. It appears to be you, Mr ..."

"Endicott."

"Thank you."

I was pleased by his courtesy.

"And your name is?"

"Culadar."

"I beg you pardon?"

"Culadar."

"Just Culadar?"

"Yes."

"I see."

Languidly, he reached forwards to shake my hand. His fingers felt like ice. After this small formality, he took his pipe and lit it. I looked around. The room still bore all the hallmarks of neglect – liver-spotted wallpaper, mottled by candlelight, and ugly, ill-used furniture arranged discordantly around its edges.

"Sammy was a slovenly creature." The man seemed to be reading my mind. "But then, this is not the Ritz, is it?"

He laughed horribly. It was a wheezing intake of breath, like a death-rattle.

"You are probably wondering where he is?"

I did not reply.

"As you know, Sammy is a native of these parts and, unfortunately, he is of conscription age. Consequently, he has made himself scarce. Extremely scarce."

The bowl of his pipe was glowing satisfactorily. He tugged on it then offered the implement to me. I declined.

"You are also probably wondering where I am from?"

His eyes widened. In truth, it was impossible to say. He had a strange accent, but it was impossible to tell what it was. His pupils focussed lazily on mine. They were hugely dilated.

"My name is an enigma. Am I a Chinaman, a Lascar, a Malay, or possibly a Romany? It is hard to tell, is it not? Many nations commingle in my veins. As far as this war is concerned," he paused in mid flow, "as you will understand, I am somewhat divided in my loyalties. But that is neither here nor there."

He must have felt that he had gained my trust. He held my gaze.

"However," he continued, "one would not like to see the war won, shall we say, unfairly." He pronounced the word carefully. "That would not be cricket, would it, Mr Endicott?" He shifted in his seat. "But I have neglected the basic courtesies. Please sit down, won't you? By the way," he gave an oily grin, "you will not be required to share a bed with me. I shall sleep on the divan."

"That is good of you ... sir."

Momentarily, I had forgotten his name.

"Not at all. The disadvantage, of course, is that the mattress contains legions of hungry bed-bugs, swollen with the blood of the previous occupant."

His shoulders heaved. I prayed that he would stop laughing soon. I got a better look at his face now. What I had taken for a shadow was actually a faint moustache. It curved around a pink, delicate mouth. Finally, his amusement subsided.

"Please, Mr Endicott, settle yourself. Make yourself as comfortable as these straitened circumstances will allow. There is a washstand." He pointed towards an obscure corner. "That, I am afraid, is the extent of the facilities."

I placed my kit-bag on the bed, removed my coat, and draped it over the iron frame. The quilt was clammy to the touch. But it was a cold night. I would need it. Bed bugs were a horror. I knew that in the morning my legs and stomach would be covered in sore red welts.

Culadar adjusted his armchair, to see me better. His physical position suggested repose. But his mind was still active.

"You said that it would be unfortunate for this war to be won, unjustly," I said, testing him.

"I did."

I sat on the bed. It adjusted to my weight, in a cacophony of springs and levers.

"What did you mean?"

"Mr Endicott, I have waited for a long time for a person to come through that door. According to the laws of chance, it could have been a mechanic, a blind piano tuner, a drayman, or a sailor degraded by syphilis. However, because I am gifted with prescience, I suspected that this would not be the case. And I was right. It was you."

He knitted his fingers together. His left thumb-nail, which he used to firm the bowl of his pipe, was long and stained.

"We are figures in the same pattern, Mr Endicott. Sammy is another part of it. So is your friend, Harold Hawkins, the journalist. I have been rewarded for my patience ... By the way, would you like a drink? Whisky is not to my taste, however, I believe that Sammy may have laid some down in his, cellar."

I shrugged. The prospect did not fill me with glee. However, it would have been rude to refuse his offer.

Remembering my previous visit to this room, I crossed to the wardrobe. At its base, beneath some vile rags, was a greasy bottle. I hoped that the jaundiced liquid it contained was a product of distillation.

"There is a tumbler on the washstand."

"Thank you. Would you care to join me?"

"No, Mr Endicott. The poppy and the malt make poor bed-fellows I fear." His shoulders vibrated, as strange sounds issued from his windpipe. I resumed my position on the bed, waiting for the death-rattle to subside.

"Where was I? Ah yes, the war. It has become clear, as you know, that a stalemate now exists that will not easily be broken. The opposing armies have buried themselves into the mud, like colonies of termites. Their scientists and military engineers are constantly devising new methods of mutilation and torture – flame throwers, mines, poison gas – but the two forces are exquisitely balanced. Neither side can gain a decisive advantage.

"However, that state would no longer exist if one side possessed a new order of weapon. For example, an explosive device of unparalleled strength. Perhaps, for example, a weapon derived from the energy that resides in matter itself."

"A uranium bomb," I said.

"Precisely."

He did not flinch.

"Its possessors – at least if they were blessed with organisational and tactical skills – would not necessarily unleash it on the battle field, or even close to the battle field. They might choose a famous landmark or monument to destroy. Something of huge significance. Something that the world would miss."

"Like the Great Pyramid?"

"Indeed."

He stroked his chin.

"I believe that we are thinking along the same lines, Mr Endicott. Is it possible that we have seen some of the same documents?"

I tried to look non-committal.

"But here's the thing." He tilted his head. "I happen to know that they, the conspirators, have moved on from their Egyptian scheme, in which they have been thwarted by the vagaries of the weather, compounded by human failure. They now have a target in view that is far more significant."

"Really? May I ask you what it is?"

He blinked.

"Can I trust you, Mr Endicott?"

Could he trust me? I had crossed a continent on the brink of war and had risked death in a strange land, I had been banged up in Wandsworth jail and frozen and blasted in the trenches. I had learnt to fly. And I had crossed Kent on foot, sleeping in ditches. I said nothing. The expression on my face must have spoken volumes.

He raised an eyebrow.

"Mr Endicott, you have established your credentials. For that I am grateful. You appear to be a resourceful young man. But I must tell you that the next stage in this business is fraught with danger. As you know, the people we are up against are ruthless. Extremely ruthless. They are armed to the teeth and they do not take prisoners. The stakes are far too high for that. Do you think you are up to the task?"

I sighed.

I was beginning to lose patience with his hints and riddles.

"I am very tired," I said. "Really, if there is no more ..."

He took a breath.

"Mr Endicott, are you familiar with the River Ouse?"

The question brought to mind a geography lesson, decades before.

"It is in East Sussex, I think. It cuts through the South Downs."

"That is correct. Well, next to the Ouse is a pretty village, called Rodmell. It lies halfway between Lewes and Newhaven. And to the north of the village is a manor house."

"So?"

"That is where you must go. All I can say, at this juncture, is that there is something close to that house that will be of great interest to you. That is probably all you need to know. I do not wish to frighten you."

I felt foolish at my earlier outburst.

"I'm sorry if I ..."

"That is quite all right."

"You must be more than ready for your ... bed."

We both laughed.

"And you for your divan."

"Opium is a powerful sedative, Mr Endicott. I shall be as comfortable as a princess upon a feather mattress."

"Then I shall not feel guilty for taking the bed."

I raised my glass.

After I had downed its disgusting contents, I eased myself into the bedclothes. I hoped that the warmth of my body would soon dissipate their dampness and cold whilst not absorbing them. I rested against the bed-head for a while, thinking. Culadar did not extinguish the candle immediately. To my surprise, he re-filled his pipe and lit it. I was feeling light-headed. I realised that the opium fumes had insinuated themselves into my brain. It was not an unpleasant sensation.

At length, without shifting my position, I began to drift off. Was I awake or asleep? A subtle euphoria had filled my being, from my tingling scalp to the tips of my fingers. I realised that I had become hyper-sensitive to light. The candle was glowing like a magnificent sun. And tendrils of bright smoke were oscillating around Culadar's head. They were forming, like twists of yarn, a coherent shape. It struck me – it was my last conscious thought – that I had seen something like this before, in Transylvania – a creature, with a swan's neck, hooded eyes and crenellated wings. The smoke had resolved itself into an image of perfect clarity. It was a dragon.

When I woke up, just after dawn, Culadar had gone. The strange thing is, there was no sign that he had ever occupied the room. I scoured my surroundings, remembering the tiniest details of our conversation. At least the shape of the next day or two was clear. I must go to East Sussex and follow his instructions. The thought cheered me up. And the weather matched my mood. It seemed a little brighter.

The landlady was extremely vexed that I was leaving her delightful establishment so soon. Needless to say, she refused to reimburse any portion of my five shillings. I left her on a perplexing note. I asked her when a man with long black hair and yellow skin had moved into the room I had just left. From my description, he must have sounded like the celebrated fictional character, Fu Manchu.

"What?"

She squinted at me alarmingly.

"There ain't been no such man. Not in my 'ouse. I don't like foreigners. That room 'as been empty these past four weeks, as Gawd is my witness."

She propelled me across the threshold. It was a relief to breathe fresh, rain-scented air. I bade her farewell as the front door slammed and made my way down Fournier Street, feeling almost jaunty.

"Hello. Katie?"

"Austin!"

She sounded astonished to hear my voice. Hers was faint. Telephones were fairly primitive in those days and one generally had to shout into them. People still regarded them as a kind of witchcraft.

"Where are you?"

I looked around me.

"I would rather not say."

"I see."

There was a pause.

"Well, how are you?"

"I am very well. Never better. I slept last night in a comfortable bed and I have had a good breakfast."

I was speaking the truth. My stomach and shins were bitten to blazes and itching. But the bed bugs had been a small price to pay for what I had learnt in Fournier Street. After leaving Sammy the Shim's, I had drifted towards the West End. I had loitered for most of the day in nooks and crannies. In the late afternoon, I had begged the proprietor of a shirt shop in New Bond Street to let me use his telephone. I was an anxious father, I lied, whose daughter was ill.

Eventually, he gave in. I had called up the operator and

asked to be connected to the Prince's Theatre, knowing that Katie normally arrived at five o'clock, to prepare for her evening performance.

"What happened after ... you know," I said, enigmatically.

"The beastly man in the red cap was taken to hospital."

"Was he well enough to question you first?"

"Yes."

Shame, I thought. I should have plugged him. One in the chest, two in the head.

"Katie, did you give him your address?"

"I'm afraid so, Austin, yes."

"Your real address?"

"Of course."

She seemed shocked that I had wanted her to tell a lie. And she was an actress! Damn, I thought. I should not be able to go back to her rooms.

"Never mind. I understand." I cleared my throat. "Listen, Katie, there has been a development. I have received a new piece of information. And I must go somewhere."

"Really? Where?"

"I cannot tell you. But it is a nice place, in the countryside. I am quite looking forward to it."

"Can I come?"

"No."

"Austin?" She sounded hurt. "Please can I come?"

"No. It is far too dangerous."

"Oh, Austin."

She was incredibly persistent.

"What about the play?" I said.

"It is coming off after tonight. Last night, we played to only three people. And two of those were Ethel Smyth."

She giggled. The joke, I speculated, would already be making its way across London.

"Please, let me come with you, Austin."

"No. Under no circumstances."

In the end, I gave in. Women always get their way in the end. It is an ineluctable law of nature. Her company would be pleasant, I reflected. At least if we were not killed.

"Where shall we meet?"

I named the first place that came into my head.

"By the statue of Eros, at ten o'clock, tomorrow morning."

Brilliant, Austin, I told myself, later. Somewhere really inconspicuous. Piccadilly Circus!

"Excellent."

As far as she was concerned, the matter was dealt with. She did not give me time to have second thoughts.

"Good bye, Austin."

"Good bye."

I replaced the receiver.

"Have you finished, sir?"

The owner of the shop was hovering in the doorway.

"Yes, thank you."

"I hope that your daughter is ..."

"She appears to be making a full recovery."

I smiled at him. He seemed content. I had not realised before how easy it was to deceive people by lying. But then, look at the war.

I put my hand in my pocket.

"Please sir." He raised his palm, like a policeman. "There is no charge."

That night, I slept out in one of London's private squares. Ironically, the place was very close to the Exhibition Rooms. Initially, the main problem was the cold. I put on all of my clothes, wrapped myself in the groundsheet and made a kind of nest, in a bank of wet leaves. But it was still freezing. It began to rain, right on cue, just after midnight.

Noises, even if they are innocent in origin, can assume a

terrifying dimension when one is sleeping out at night. And dogs, with their natural curiosity, are the vagrant's worst enemy. I spent the whole night clutching my dagger. I was virtually crying with relief when I realised, from the twittering of birds, that dawn was imminent. My knees and elbows had locked; I was only a few notches, on the scale of discomforture, from hypothermia.

I had a little money left. I must now find an all-night café, the kind frequented by cheerful bummarees and inebriated cab drivers, and revive myself with a steaming mug of sweet tea. Smithfield Market would be a good bet. I was praying, as I levered myself over the iron railings, that no policeman would stop me.

Chapter Seventeen

Katie was an intensely practical creature. And she had thought carefully about her clothes. She was wearing a heavy loose-sleeved coat, with a fur-trimmed collar; beneath it were a short skirt, coming up to her calves, and a pair of sturdy shoes. Her cheek, which she presented me to kiss, was very cold.

Piccadilly Circus is not an ideal meeting place on a Saturday morning. First, we must find each other, amidst the soldiers and their sweethearts, then fight our way through the trams, buses and cabs that flew at us from all directions, to get to the entrance of the tube station. I told Katie that we should be taking the underground railway to Arsenal; after that, I said there would be a bit of route march. I did not say where we were going. Katie seemed content. She settled into a dream-like state as the packed train rattled beneath Covent Garden. Two military policemen alighted at Russell Square. I looked down, hoping for the best.

We walked down Gillespie Road making a strange couple. Katie's natural instinct was to draw attention to herself. Her quietness seemed unnatural; I sensed that she was playing the role of a runaway as we walked along. It was a dull morning. The sky was as grey as lead and a thin rain was falling. I had not properly dried out since the previous night and my boots were squelching. I hoped that Katie had remembered to bring some money, because I was now down to a handful of coins.

"You can talk you know."

"Sorry, Austin. Where are we going?"

"To Highbury Corner. My old house."

"Why?"

"It's a bit of a secret. A surprise."

"A nice one?"

"I hope so."

I had moved into the house after I had received my father's

161

substantial inheritance, in 1913. It was a large property for a single man – a Victorian villa with a bay-windowed front. Behind the house was a small mews. Here were some work-shops and stables, one of which I rented. The stable was home to something that I valued highly – my pride and joy.

There is a public house just north of Highbury Corner. I asked Katie to wait there. The next stage was somewhat perilous; it was possible, although unlikely, that my house was being watched. I had no intention of entering it, but I must pass behind it, to reach the mews. The stable door was padlocked; the key was hidden beneath a flagstone. I pushed open the wooden door with a feeling of dread. But it was there! Meagre daylight revealed a long, rectangular object, reaching to my waist. Smiling, I removed a grey dust-sheet and uncovered my treasured possession – a Singer 10 motor car.

The 1,100 CC, open-topped two-seater had been very latest thing when I had bought it – much to my brother's disgust – in 1913. For its weight and size, it was one of the fastest cars on the road. The car had been well-maintained and was in pristine condition. Just touching its dark blue bonnet made me feel excited. Hitherto, I had only driven the vehicle as far as Burnham Beeches. This journey would be far more challenging.

The tank was full and there was a spare can of petrol in the boot. But would the car start? I would have to turn on the fuel tap, disengage the clutch, adjust the throttle, prime the carburettor, and perform several other complicated tasks, before even touching the starting handle. If the engine misfired, the handle would give a nasty kick, which could break my arm.

The look of shock on Katie's face was priceless when she recognised my face. She broke into a grin, as I stopped and helped her onto the running board. Later, she told me that she had never been in a motor car before. I warned her that the wind would buffet and deafen us and that we would soon be as cold as Eskimos and gave her a blanket to put on her lap. In no time, we were zipping down Upper Street, weaving between the tramlines.

The car turned heads and once Katie felt reassured that she would not be flung out, she started to enjoy herself – the main problem was the titanic battle between the wind and her hair. A notion now came to me that made me happy. Once I was out of London, I should be able to ignore the speed limit and there was unlikely to be anything on the road that could travel faster. Soon, we would be out of the realm of top-heavy trams and lumbering motor buses and I could open up the throttle.

I have always loved the view from Blackfriars Bridge. I looked first at the Houses of Parliament, rising from the mists that wreathed the brown river, then at Katie. She seemed to read my thoughts. We, and Harry, were now batting for Britain – its freedoms and treasured institutions were in our hands. We were perhaps the only people on the planet who could preserve them. I should not have felt so pleased with myself. I should have remembered that hubris always leads to downfall.

South of the river, the Walworth Road was jammed with mainly horse-driven traffic. We slowed down to a crawl. After Brixton, we passed through a succession of suburbs that I had barely heard of – interminable streets of dull, brown houses and faded shops. It was not until Purley that that the ugly sprawl of London definitively petered out. Helped by an oil-stained road atlas, we now located the East Grinstead Road. This would take us most of the way to Rodmell.

It was a great relief to see green fields, nibbled by horses and sheep, rising above the rooftops. I now managed to get the car into third gear. Katie was pushed backwards as we reached an astonishing speed – thirty-five miles per hour! Bending towards the driver's seat, she tried to say something to me. I could not hear her but I nodded and smiled. Perhaps a small part of me was showing off. It is not an attractive character trait. We were whizzing through Warlingham, when Katie tugged at my sleeve.

"Austin!" I heard my name above the roar of the wind. She was pointing behind her. I looked back. I saw what had alarmed her – a sleek, black two-seater, with a wedge-shaped radiator. Katie shouted in my ear, indicating that the car was following us. She could not have known it, but it was a Vauxhall Prince Henry! A Prince Henry had clocked more than seventy miles per hour at Brooklands – we did not have a chance of outrunning it.

Looking back again, I saw that the driver and his passenger were wearing leather helmets and flying goggles. The passenger pointed at me. His leather gauntlet flared out at the wrist. I gulped. Only the police wore gloves like that. It seemed scarcely credible, but a policeman must have followed Katie on foot from Covent Garden, pursued us to Highbury, then alerted a motorised detachment of the Metropolitan Police, or perhaps Special Branch, by telephone.

The Vauxhall was gaining on my little Singer every second. The denouement was inevitable. It would overtake and force me to stop. If only ... I reached into my jacket. The Webley was loaded with a full cylinder. I have said that I am an exceptional shot. For what I was to do next, I would need to be.

"Take the wheel, Katie!" The urgency of my command alarmed her. She did the necessary and gripped the steering wheel with her kid gloves. As I twisted in my seat, the Singer swerved violently, almost landing us in a ditch. The Vauxhall was now only twenty yards from our bumper. I could see the tense expression on the driver's white face. Katie corrected the car's line as I drew my weapon. She was already getting the hang of steering. That's the spirit, girl. I levelled the barrel and aligned the sights. The driver stiffened in his seat. He looked surprised. The first bullet shattered the Vauxhall's windscreen – exactly as I had intended. The next target would be more difficult. It took three more shots. I had the great satisfaction of seeing one of the Vauxhall's front tyres burst and of watching the driver wrestle with the wheel, as the car lurched off the road.

Only Katie saw what happened next. The car flipped onto its side and both men were flung out. One of them was moving, she said; the other lay still. Soon, they were tiny black dots. It was not hard to imagine Roman legions clomping along this road. We picked up speed as it descended, bordered by thick hawthorn hedges. At the bottom of the incline, it crossed a stone bridge and ran, as straight as a carpenter's rule, through a sodden water meadow, towards East Grinstead.

Good grief. Nobody should see what I was seeing. Certainly not a young lady. How was I going to describe it to Katie? I was standing on tiptoe, peering through a window. We had found Northease Manor easily enough. It was set back from the road just to the north of Rodmell, a two-storey flint building with tall chimneys and a gabled entrance. To the right of the manor house, was a thatched medieval barn.

We had arrived just as dusk was falling, hidden the car down a leafy track and approached gingerly, on foot. The lights of the hall were blazing. One sensed, from the shadows dancing behind its casements, that it was full of people and movement. The gravel drive, which was disfigured by ugly pollarded trees, was crowded with motor cars. Here, chauffeurs in peaked caps smoked and traded gossip. Katie and I were drawn, as if by gravity, to the front door.

"Listen," I said, "we've struck gold here. If I am not mistaken, this is a meeting of the Minerva League. I recognise some of these cars from Highgate."

She nodded.

"Here is the plan. You will go to the door. A footman will ask you who you are. Give him some fictitious name, and play for time."

"Such as?" She looked at me, questioningly. Sometimes, we could read each other's minds.

"I don't know," I said, "Tinkerbell. It doesn't matter. I cannot go with you, because I would be recognised. While you are trying to get in, I shall investigate the barn and perhaps have a snoop around the back. We'll meet back at the car in exactly one hour."

"What if the footman allows me inside, Austin?"

"He is not very likely to, without an invitation. Believe me, Ellen Terry could not talk her way into there."

My scepticism was a provocation. Before I could say more, Katie was striding towards the hall. I adjusted my posture. I must try to look as casual as possible, so as not to arouse the curiosity of the chauffeurs, who were looking at me suspiciously. In fact, I decided, I would pretend to be one of them. I lit up a Gold Flake and attempted to smoke it nonchalently. It would not be out of character for an off-duty servant to take a sly peek into the barn at the side of the house. Noise and movement were evident inside. Fringed with dark thatch, its latticed windows were glowing like orange beacons. I approached.

Inside the barn, a horrifying scene had been revealed. A man – a thin, pale-skinned specimen with a bald pate – was standing at the centre of a black and white tiled floor. A linen apron, his sole garment, only served to accentuate that which it was supposed to conceal. The man was standing behind a tethered white goat. His jaws were clenched. A dagger was held in his fist. His hand, I saw, was vibrating to a monotonous rhythm. This was coming from halberds and shields, struck on

166

the floor by men in armour. There was another sound, a floating, melodic chorus. Around the bald man, one had the impression of a blurred pink curtain. It was flesh, I realised – a wall of warbling women. And they were naked, save for wisps of white silk and helmets of beaten silver.

"'Ere, mate!"

I felt a hand on my shoulder.

"You don't want to be ..."

I looked round.

"Quite," I said. "I was only ..."

"I know what you was doing."

The man gave a ghastly wink.

"It's a right carry on, 'ain't it," he said. "I am 'ere with the Mayor of Lewes."

Was he the man who was about to ... I did not speak my thoughts.

"Who are you with, mate?"

"Er ... Lord Swaffingham," I said. It was the first name that came into my head.

"Oh." The man seemed satisfied.

I glanced at the front door of the hall. It was closed and Katie was not there.

"We was wondering ..."

The driver gestured towards his mates.

"Of course," I lied. "I should be delighted to join you."

I felt stupid, as soon as the words had left my mouth. A chauffeur would never use such effete language.

"But first, I must ..."

I pointed towards the road.

"'Ave a jimmy riddle?"

"Yes."

The man laughed. With my hands in my coat pockets, I lurched away from him down the drive, in a comic attempt to run and walk at the same time.

Katie was already waiting in the car, looking somewhat deflated. I was out of breath, uncertain whether I had been followed.

"Well?" she said. I saw the gap in her front teeth. My mother always said that this was a lucky feature in human physiognomy.

"What did you see?"

"I do not really want to say," I said. "But it was them all right."

"Who?"

"The Minerva League. Performing one of their rituals."

I looked up at the sky. The moon was full tonight.

"How do you know that it was the league?"

The naked women? The men with shields? The long-suffering goat? These were all likely indications of the organisation. I remained silent.

"Oh come on, Austin," said Katie. "I have been around, you know. I have seen *Salome*. I have even been to Bradford."

Reluctantly, I described what I had witnessed in the barn, omitting certain details. I explained that the cracked idiots who were members of the Minerva League liked to prance about in operatic costumes and that they inducted new members into their organisation by inflicting cruelty upon helpless animals. Their antics, I said, evoked the legends of the Rhine Maidens and Valhalla. But their activities were infinitely more worrying than Wagner's overblown operas.

"Why, Austin?"

Her expression could be startlingly candid.

"Because they, or their friends, have access to a bloody great bomb. And they are prepared to use it, however much destruction is caused, so that Germany will win the war."

"The one they were going to blow up the pyramids with?"

"Exactly. But that plan appears to have gone wrong."

"Where are they going to use it next?"

"I have no idea."

I felt an overwhelming urge to smoke. I had never craved a cigarette so much in my life. I fumbled in my pocket.

"What are we going to do now?"

I shrugged. I lit a Gold Flake. It was my last one.

An idea was taking shape.

"Listen ..."

It was simple. We turned the car round, so that it was facing the main road. From here, we would be able to watch as cars left the manor house, at conclusion of the meeting. We would then nudge out of the lane and follow discretely one of the vehicles, back to London. It was not much of a plan. But it was the best I could do. As we waited, the moon put in an appearance. It burst forth from from behind a chimney of the manor house. The same shining disc, I reflected, was lighting up No-Man's Land.

Chapter Eighteen

"Look, Austin!"

Katie jabbed my arm. I must have nodded off. I hated sleeping in those days. It brought to the surface of my mind all kinds of strange visitations. A stream of vehicles was leaving the hall, their headlamps stabbing the road like searchlights. I must wake myself up, jump out of the car and get it started. I was cursing. By the time I had finished, most of the visitors had gone.

I don't know why, but one of the stragglers, an open-topped four-seater like an over-sized bath-tub, caught my attention. It was a luxury car – a Lanchester. Its occupants were muffled up in heavy coats. Instead of turning north, for London, this vehicle swung the other way, southwards. An instinct spoke to me. Follow it.

I had left the engine on. I released the emergency brake, adjusted the throttle and engaged the clutch. The Lanchester did not seem to be in a hurry. I must hang back, but not allow it to get out of sight. To my great relief, the car maintained a slow, stately progress. After only half a mile, it surprised us. It turned off the Newhaven road and entered the village of Rodmell.

In those days, street-lamps were unknown in the countryside. On either side of the road, we could just make out the dim forms of cottages made of brick and tile, some with thatched roofs. In the daylight, one could not wish for a prettier English village. I held back from the Lanchester, suspecting that it would soon stop. It did. Rounding a bend, we saw that it was parked front of a weather-board cottage.

Katie knocked on the door. She was to do the talking. After all, she was the actress. There was a fumbling of bolts. I saw a lump rise in her throat.

"Hello."

The woman who had opened it was tall and slightly stooped. She wore a pale silk cocktail dress. Her hair was chestnut-coloured. Her nose was like a beak – that was the first thing one noticed about her. Her eyelids were heavy, almost like hoods, beneath quizzical eyebrows.

"Good evening. I know it is extremely late but our car has broken down and ..."

All traces of a northern accent had disappeared from Katie's voice.

The woman looked us up and down, silently appraising our social status.

"I see," she said, slowly.

"We are terribly sorry to inconvenience you. We were just wondering ..." Katie paused.

"You had better come in."

The woman turned away. She was not exactly friendly.

"You had better take off your wet things." She pointed to a row of pegs. It was the mother lode. We had struck gold! I resisted the temptation to whoop in exaltation.

There was a damp smell in the hallway, like wet dog mixed with mildew. But the sitting room was cosy enough. The flagstone floor was dotted with colourful rugs; there was an odd mixture of antique and modern furniture – all of it expensive and well-made – and modern paintings. The walls were a peculiar shade of green. I could not decide if the colour was soothing or disturbing. It was a familiar scene to me – a Bloomsbury interior of a Bohemian kind, transposed to Sussex.

Two gentlemen were present. One was standing next to a gramophone holding a record; the other was seated by the fire. The music lover was dressed from head to foot in shades of grey – he looked like a felt mouse. Only his black beard provided a note of chromatic variety. Like the woman, he had a narrow face and an aquiline nose. Artistic. It was obvious that they made up a pair. The man by the fire was older, tweedy and, from his expression, bilious. He did not get up when we entered the room. In fact, he scarcely looked at us.

"I am sorry. I don't know your names."

The dress of our hostess was haute couture. It would have cost most people a month's salary. It rippled over her haunches like a mill-stream.

Time to improvise.

"I am James Wilsona and this is my fiancee, Dora Bulstrode."

Katie suppressed a snort. Why on earth had I chosen such a hideous moniker?

I felt self-conscious. I badly needed a shave. My clothes looked as though I had slept in them. In fact, I had slept in them. Only Katie's brightness and self-confidence would get us through this.

"I see."

The fashionable lady did not smile. When upper class people have divined that you are of no interest or use to them, they dismiss you instantly; you seem to become transparent.

"My name is Hackett, Serena Hackett. This is my fiance, Guy Temple. May I also introduce," she pointed towards the fireplace, "Major Guy Neville. He is the Marquess of Abergavenny."

The man grunted. He was not that old, I saw that now. But his face had been ruined by drink. The grey mouse, Temple, moved towards us. I shook his hand.

"What line of work are you in Mr, Wilson."

"I er ... a clerk. I am an accounts clerk, for a brewery."

"Oh." He seemed infinitely disappointed.

"And Miss Bulstrode?"

"I am an actress," said Katie.

She smiled radiantly, showing the gap in her front teeth.

"Oh, really?" He brightened. "Are you in anything at the moment?"

I touched her foot with mine. Make something up, I thought, for God's sake, Katie.

"Well, I was in *The Boatswain's Mate*, you know the musical by Ethel Smyth, at the Prince's Theatre."

"In one of the principal roles?"

"Not exactly. I ..."

"We know Miss Smyth very well." Serena Hackett cut off Katie in mid-flow. "In fact, she was down here for luncheon, only last weekend."

I recalled the peculiar apparition of the woman in spats, in the alleyway behind the theatre.

"Ethel is certainly a ... character."

We were all content with Guy Temple's euphemism. And we had now established a tenuous social connection. The atmosphere lightened.

"What is your occupation, Mr Temple?"

"Oh." He seemed surprised by my question. "I am a hack. I write for various high-minded magazines that you will never have heard of. Sometimes, I am allowed to write books. But, in this regard, I am not nearly as successful as Serena. Have you heard of *The Siren's Song*? That was her first novel." He looked admiringly at his wife. "Rave reviews. Do you know, she actually gets letters from admirers, from all over the world!"

"Guy!" The woman's expression could have frozen a pail of water. If there is one thing that wealthy people do not like – the truly wealthy – it is boastfulness.

Temple looked guilty, like a child caught stealing. He had an idea.

"We were just about to have a night cap, Mr Wilson. Would you care to join us?"

I tried to hide my enthusiasm.

"I am not sure, the hour is very late and ..."

"Oh come. Please." He looked at me imploringly. His eyes

were deep brown, like a Spaniel's.

"Well, if you insist."

"Splendid!"

One could sense, from her demeanour, that the lady author was displeased by her husband's invitation.

"Whisky and soda?"

"Yes, please."

"Take a seat with the marquess, Mr Wilson." He winked. "He hates it when I call him that. The ladies can fend for themselves, I think."

The man by the fire was in a dreamy world of his own. His eyes were rheumy and bloodshot. He looked at me like a startled animal.

"Are you over there?" he said, suddenly, in a distracted voice.

"I'm sorry?"

"In France?"

"No," I lied. "But I am just about to get my papers, I expect. I am anxious to serve my country."

"Take my advice."

He leaned towards me.

"And what is that?"

"Don't!" He guffawed, unpleasantly.

I did not know how to react. The uneasy silence that followed was broken by Guy Temple, bearing down on us with drinks.

He spoke. "Take no notice of the major, Mr Wilson. His disillusionment borders on nihilism. Of course, he does know what he is talking about. The trenches and so forth – unlike the rest of us."

"Tell me, have you answered the call of your country, Mr Temple?" I said.

"God, no." He frowned. "Being shouted at, not changing one's socks. Not for me, I'm afraid. When the time comes, if it comes, they will have to drag me kicking and screaming all the way. However," he smiled mysteriously, "I suspect that I shall be spared that fate. I have certain friends, you see ..."

"Really?" I said.

The major cleared this throat. This sound indicated that his glass was empty. Temple substituted it immediately with a tumbler of neat whisky.

"What is your regiment, major?" I said.

"The Royal Sussex," he replied.

"You must ask him if he has seen action," said Temple. "He is far too modest to tell you himself. The major was shot up by the Boche at Ypres."

The soldier's legs were covered by a tartan blanket. I now saw that one of them was sticking out at an odd angle. The poor fellow's hands were trembling. His nerves were shot. But it was whisky that would kill him now, not Germans.

The major contemplated his glass.

"I am tired of this war, Mr ..."

"Wilson."

"Of course, I served my country. It is in the blood of the Nevilles to serve. But I do not think we should have become involved."

"Why shouldn't we?" I said.

"Mr Wilson." He looked at me. "Who would you rather have in your house, a German, or a Frenchie?"

"I don't know, I ..."

"The Frenchie is an indolent, garlic-eating scoundrel. As a fighting man, he is a about as much use as a cat in a thunderstorm. But your Saxon ..." his eyes seemed to sparkle. "We are of the same blood, Wilson. We should never have fought them. And now our two countries are bleeding each other death. It is a scandal."

Temple giggled. Everything was a game to him.

"But surely," I said, "we Britons are of French descent just as much as German?"

The major shot me a venomous glance. His cheeks were purple. I looked across the room. Katie and Serena Hackett were conversing. They did not seem relaxed. Behind them was a small Georgian writing desk. Periodicals with parchment-coloured covers lay upon it. These would be the magazines that Temple wrote for – weird conflations, I suspected, of literature, economic science and philosophy. Katie, or I, must examine, as soon as possible, the contents of that desk.

"I can see your point of view, major," I said.

"But you do not share it?"

"Well, I am about to take the king's shilling, I can hardly ..."

"Exactly. Kitchener, not the Kaiser!" Temple broke in. "Major, you are upsetting Mr Wilson. The poor man is terrified by your opinions."

"Kitchener!" exclaimed the major. I have never heard a person utter a name with such distaste. "He has taken our lads – the cream of England – and led them to the slaughter, like sheep. He is not the man that you think he is, you know!" He glared at the fire.

"What do you mean?" I said.

"Come, major," said Temple. "Don't you think that you have shocked our guest enough, without impugning one of our country's bravest heroes?"

The major made a noise. It lay halfway between a grunt and a growl. He had already emptied his glass. Surely, he wasn't going to down another one? Temple picked up the cue. He crossed at once to the drinks cabinet. He was killing the major, just as surely as German artillery. The major crooked his finger. I leaned towards him. His breath smelled like the bottom of a barrel. He spoke *sotto voice*.

"He wears women's drawers you know."

"Who does?"

He did not answer. I never found out whether he was referring to Lord Kitchener or to Guy Temple. He breathed stale whisky into my ear.

"Wilson, we are talking big words tonight. But it does not matter. None of it matters. Do you know why?"

I shook my head.

He placed a hand on my thigh. "Because, my boy, something is going to happen – tomorrow night, on the stroke of midnight. Something very important. Something that will change everything."

"What?"

On the other side of the room, Temple was conversing with his wife.

"I should not be telling you about Operation Raven. It is the whisky talking. But, let me put it this way. Boom!" He slapped his good leg, grinning like an idiot.

"An explosion?"

He placed a finger on his lips.

"Vowed to silence. But, if I were you ..." Temple was coming towards us now, "I would avoid London, for the next couple of days."

"I'm afraid that this will have to be your last drink, major." Temple held out a full glass.

"Really?"

"Yes. Serena is rather tired. It has been a long evening. Mr Wilson," he paused, "I have had a thought."

"What is that?"

"How would you and your fiancée like to stay here tonight? We have lots of room. You can sort out your motor in the morning. The village blacksmith can take a look at it. He is an excellent man."

"Really, we couldn't."

"How can you refuse? Besides, where else would you go? This is Rodmell, you know, not the Strand." He smiled.

"Well, if you insist ..."

He was falling right into my hands, I thought. It was easy.

"Good man."

He said something to the major. I was not listening. Time seemed to have slowed. Temple's white, fire-licked face moved soundlessly. Was he one of the men whom I had seen in the barn, beating their spears on the floor as the naked women chanted? I seemed to hear the women's unearthly voices ringing through my head and the thudding of the weapons, like jungle drums.

"Darling!"

Serena Hackett's voice broke through my reverie. She seemed annoyed.

"It is after one!"

"Of course. Mr Wilson, that was the authentic siren's song. I believe that we have been summoned to bed. I hope that you will be comfortable in your rooms. Do you have overnight things?"

"Not really. I have a small bag. It is in the car. Do you mind if I fetch it?"

"Of course not."

He waited for me. When I came back into the living room with my kit-bag, the major was snoring like an old dog by the fire. I wondered where he would sleep. Serena Hackett gave Katie and me a cold look and said goodnight without enthusiasm. Temple seemed embarrassed. He led us up the stairs.

"Well, Katie, what do you think?"

I had crept into her room, about an hour after we had gone to bed. We talked softly.

"Of what?"

"Of our hosts?"

She wrinkled her nose.

"Serena Hackett is horrible. She is a frightful snob. When I told her I was from Huddersfield she looked at me as if I had murdered someone. What do you suppose her novel is like, Austin?"

"A lot of tosh about nymphs and fauns, I expect, tricked out with some modern profanity. What did you make of Temple?"

Katie smiled.

"Did you see his shoes?"

"No, why?"

"They were extraordinary – more like a woman's than a man's shoes."

"I did not notice them."

We heard a fox bark. The room's curtains were open. The cottage's back garden, which could be seen through the window, was substantial. At the end of it, was a dark mass – the square tower and pointed spire of an ancient church.

"These people in the Minerva League, are certainly a queer lot, Katie," I said. "I have been around a bit, you know. But even so ... I can't wait to tell Harry about all this."

She looked down. "You were talking to that major for a long time."

"He had a lot to say."

"About what?"

"Mainly rubbish. But he told me something amazing. He just let it slip out, when Temple wasn't listening. He told me about Operation Raven."

"Operation Raven?"

"Poetic isn't it?"

I looked through the window. The moon slipped from behind a cloud. Its sharp white light picked out the church's spire, so that one could almost make out individual tiles. A thought popped into my head.

"Katie," I said, "where do raven's live?"

"At the Tower of London."

179

"And what will happen to our country, if the ravens ever leave there?"

"Something absolutely dreadful."

"I have just worked it out. I know what the Minerva League are going to do. They are going to blow up the Tower of London!"

The more I thought about it, the more likely it seemed. The Tower would be relatively easy to attack. And a bomb in that part of London would have the great advantage of leaving the city's vital infrastructure intact. It would not be logical for the plotters to destroy Parliament or Buckingham Palace; after all, they would be needed, when, or if, the Minerva League took over.

"Damn it, Katie. These people are fiends!" I clenched the windowsill.

"When are they going to do it?"

"Tomorrow night, I think. That's what the major suggested."

"We don't have very much time."

"No, we don't"

"What are we going to do?"

I studied the shadowy garden. It would be lovely in the summer – drifts of delphiniums and zinnia, stately hollyhocks, clouds of sapphire-coloured forget-me-nots.

"A little later," I said, "I shall go downstairs. There is a writing desk in the sitting room. It may contain documents incriminating our friends. If that is so, I shall 'borrow' them. In the morning, we shall go back to London."

"And then?"

"I don't know."

Very likely, I would be arrested as a deserter as soon as I presented myself to the authorities. Katie would have a little more credibility. However, people would think that we were both mad.

"At least we have Harry's documents," I said, "and if we can get some more proof ..." I tried to sound positive. As I spoke, the moon vanished, like a hare diving for cover. I looked at Katie, attempting to smile.

Old houses at night produce a curious repertoire of mysterious creaks and groans, especially when one is creeping about in the dark. Dawn was a long way off. The stairs were as black as pitch. In the sitting room, I would risk lighting a lamp. I groped my way across the room. I found the desk. It was a compact, useful item, with little compartments for stamps and envelopes. Here was where the incriminating documents might be. There was a sound behind me, like a stick snapping. I turned. Framed by light in the doorway was a figure. My heart jumped. Its arm was extended. At the end of it, something was pointing in my direction. A pistol.

"May I ask what you are doing?"

"Nothing. I was just ..."

"Going through my papers."

"Of course not! If that's what it appear to be then ..."

"I am not a fool." There was a steely tone in Temple's voice. "I never liked the look of you, I must say, or that 'actress'. Well, you have confirmed my worst fears."

"I ..."

"Move away from the desk."

He jerked the barrel of his gun.

"Look," I said, "let's not ..."

"My good friend," he sneered, "you may have taken on a little more than you bargained for."

There was a bang. I felt a stinging sensation. It was the second time in my life that I had been shot. This time, it was my leg.

Chapter Nineteen

I stared straight into his eyes. I did not dare to look away. A sharp pain was pulsing through my thigh. I could feel warm liquid spreading into my trousers. If the bullet had connected with a vein or an artery, that was it; I would bleed to death. Temple's mouth was twisted into a sadistic smile. I realised two things – first, that he was going to kill me and, second, that he would enjoy it. My options were limited – dive to one side or straight at him. The odds were not that good. He was about twelve feet away. Perfect range for a pistol. There was not much time. I kept my gaze on his unblinking eyes, feeling the blood drain from my face. This was it. Three, two, one ...

There was a burst of light – it was a muzzle flash from somewhere about Temple's head – and a sharp crack. Temple cursed as he span comically, crashing into a wall. I looked up. Katie was floating like an apparition at the top of the stairs. She was holding my Webley. She looked as though she had been plugged into the mains. The gun was pointing at an odd angle – the recoil had almost jerked her arm off. But it had done its job. Whether by accident or design, she had shot Temple in the foot.

Temple had lost his weapon; it must have been flung from his grasp. He was terrified by his injury. He started to moan softly.

"Katie," I said, calmly. "Well done. Come down slowly and give me the gun."

She did. With the Webley's warm handle in my grasp, I felt a surge of power pass down my arm. I aimed it directly at the Temple's head. His body was twisted into a strange shape, like a rag doll thrown down by an impatient child.

"Now, find his gun, would you. It is over there, I think."

Katie investigated the shadows with her shoes. Temple was not looking at me now. He was blubbing like a baby. Katie's foot connected with a hard object. It was a Luger – a German service pistol. The Luger was a well-liked weapon during the war. Some British officers used to carry them.

"Thank you."

I slipped the gun into my pocket. There was a clink as it touched the Blood Stone. I groaned as a sensation like a hot, sharp blade sliced through my thigh. I looked down.

"Oh no."

Blood had saturated the fabric around the entry wound, which was marked by a small neat hole in my trousers. The bullet had made more of a mess on its way out. On its brief journey, it had sliced through some fat and a muscle or two. The pain was dreadful. However, the quantity of blood that I was losing was encouraging – it was a steady, even flow, rather than a gushing fountain. A man in the trenches seeing such a wound might have cried with joy.

"That was a damn good shot, Katie."

"Thank you." She smiled, modestly.

We heard a noise. It came from the other side of the sitting room, where ashes were glowing in a grate. It was a throaty, phlegm-filled cough. The major was waking up. The man had consumed more than a pint of whisky and had a false leg. He should not be too much of a threat.

"Major Neville!"

He spluttered an incoherent protest.

"Come over here!"

"I am not used to ..."

"I don't give a fig what you are used to!" (I did not actually use the word fig, but one that was current in the trenches.)

"Come over here. Now!"

He stumbled across the room, holding his blanket. I told him to drop it. I would need to see his hands.

"You will stand or sit next to Temple. I don't care which. If you make an unexpected move, I will kill you. Do you understand?"

The major nodded. Death was something that he was used to.

"Now, Katie." A hideous sensation sheared into my groin. "Go and fetch her ladyship from her boudoir, she will be cowering behind the door, I expect. Bring her down here."

Katie trotted up the stairs. The major's eyes followed her. Temple had no interest other than the sodden mess that had once been his fashionable shoe. An inspiration came to me. There was a structure at the bottom of the garden – a large summerhouse. After a certain amount of protest, Katie managed to establish the whereabouts of the key from the lady novelist. It was hanging on a hook in the kitchen.

Katie made a tourniquet for my thigh, using a dressing gown cord. Then we corralled our little group through the back door. I aimed my gun at them, swivelling awkwardly on my good leg, like the point of a pair of compasses. Temple's foot was certainly in a bad way; it left a trail of blood all the way down the garden path. He bleated that he would die if he did not get help. I told him not to be a fool. Even the major looked at him with contempt. Serena Hackett insisted on wearing a fur coat over her night-dress. She did not say a word.

The mission ended with the trio locked successfully in the summerhouse. Feeling like a pirate, I told them that if they tried to escape I would shoot them, without hesitation. Temple had left the world of the living; the major could hardly stand up. For her part, I knew that the lady novelist would be far too proud to do anything as vulgar or awkward as climbing through a window.

One problem was solved. But our situation did not look all that hopeful. The main thing was, I could not drive now. Without a trip to hospital, my prognosis was poor.

"Austin?" Katie said, "do you suppose that they knew we were not who we said we were?"

I winced. I was trying not to look at my thigh.

"Of course they did. I have been thinking about it. I would lay a wager that Temple knew that we were following his car from Northease Manor. It was pretty obvious."

"So, he was just pretending to believe our story."

"Of course and he probably suspected that we knew about the Minerva League."

"In which case ..."

"He lured us into staying in this house for the night, so that he could ..."

"Kill us?" Katie looked shocked.

"I think so. I believe that he was lying awake in his room. Had he not disturbed me in the sitting room, I think that he would have shot both of us, in cold blood. I could see it in his expression. Our lives meant nothing to him. Less than nothing."

Tears sprang from her eyes. She began to sob, as if she would never stop. I don't think that she was just crying for me or herself; a lot of it was for Harry. I took her in my arms, just as I had in Covent Garden, and began to coo soothing words. It was half past seven and still dark. At the foot of the stairs was a telephone. Soon, I would use it.

"Katie?"

She sniffed.

"What, Austin?"

"I have just had a thought."

"Oh yes. What is that?"

"Let's have a cup of tea."

Her mood brightened.

"There might even be some bread," I said. "Hot buttered toast would be nice."

"You would like jam, I suppose?"

"If it's not too much trouble."

She went into the kitchen. My wound, which was now wrapped in sodden towels, had not bled for some time. But the pain had been getting worse for the past hour or so. It was just bearable if I gritted my teeth. From my position, I could see the back door. My Webley was close at hand. Katie had begged me for the Luger and, with strong reservations, I had given it to her. The weapon fitted neatly into her handbag. I said she could keep it. One day, she would be able to show it to her grand-children.

After locking our hosts in the summerhouse, we had, of course, eagerly searched the writing desk. To our great disappointment, it had contained nothing of interest – not a single document referring to the Minerva League. There were only some bills and a sheath of poems, written on yellow paper. I read out one of them to Katie. We could not make head nor tail of it.

"Let me explain again."

The man at the other end of the telephone was surprisingly patient, considering what he was listening to.

"This will seem exceedingly curious to you, but please, bear me out."

"Yes ..." He lingered over the word.

"What I have to say concerns the Tower of London. You see, I believe that a bomb has been planted there. A very powerful one. It has been put there by agents of Germany. I do not know exactly where it is within the building. But this bomb will occupy a large volume. It will look like a land-mine, I should think – a large quantity of a grey mineral, with a core of dynamite. The bomb will be detonated at midnight tonight. The explosion will pulverise the Tower. There will be nothing left of it. It will also carry off Tower Bridge, I expect, and much of ..."

"Sir?"

"Yes ..."

The man was a desk officer, at Scotland Yard. A sergeant. I had been unable to talk to anyone of higher rank.

"Where did you find out this information?"

"I cannot tell you. That is, I could. But it would be a long story. Many people are involved."

"I see."

I sensed that I was losing him.

"Listen, all I am asking you to do, is to telephone the Tower. They will know if anything unusual has been reported in the past few days. Someone will need to conduct a thorough, room-by-room search. Better still, you should send some men over there. Ideally ..."

"Thank you sir."

My time was up.

"So you will look into this?"

"Yes, sir. I have taken down the details. Believe me, we will give this matter our full attention."

I could almost see him winking.

"Remember, at midnight ..."

"Thank you. Good morning."

He terminated the conversation. At that moment, Katie appeared. She was carrying a tray. Struggling beneath the burden of a large brown teapot, cups, saucers and plates, she was grinning like a Cheshire cat.

"Guess what, Austin?"

"What?"

"I found some jam. It is damson I think."

I smiled weakly. My face was filmed with sweat. I didn't have the heart to tell her, but I hated damson jam. Hot tea has marvellous therapeutic properties. It did not remove the pain that was pullulating through my thigh, but it certainly helped. We laughed at the thought of the lady novelist, the grey mouse and the mad major, locked together in the summerhouse.

"What do you think will happen, Austin?"

I pondered the question.

"The village doctor whom I have just telephoned will arrive shortly. He will probably want to call the police when he arrives, seeing that I have suffered a gunshot wound."

"Should we tell the police about them?" She jerked her thumb towards the back door.

I frowned.

"To be honest, I don't care."

"But they might die in there, Austin."

She looked at me imploringly.

"I don't think so. It is only a shed."

I remembered my prison cell in Wandsworth. I had paced it at night, trying to stop my muscles from wasting away. Our current situation was not bright. Soon, in all probability, I would be incarcerated again. I was sure that the man at Scotland Yard had not believed a word of my story.

"Katie."

"Yes?"

"I think that we should leave here, as soon as possible. It is far too dangerous for us to stay."

"But surely ..." She looked down.

I tried to lift my leg. Blood had spread around my body, forming a sticky pool. Was I strong enough? I felt sick and weak. Katie edged forwards to help me. Suddenly, there was an almighty crash. I knew what it was – the police smashing through the front door. One of the trio in the summerhouse must have broken out and sounded the alarm. The men flowed through the house like a pack of hounds. Soon, one of them – a huge man, with a black moustache – was training a gun on me. Katie protested loudly. She had never been arrested before. In less than five minutes, we had been hand-cuffed and pushed through the front door.

Chapter Twenty

Captain Stokes was a surprise. He was taller and thinner than his colleague in Special Branch, Gribley; in fact, he was almost cadaverous. However, his demeanour was cheerful and positive. And, unlike Gribley, he was not afflicted with bad breath.

"Do you smoke, Endicott?" he said.

Without hesitation, I said yes. Being locked up changes one's habits a great deal. He pulled a silver case from his jacket and flipped open the lid. Beneath a silk band, were expensive Turkish cigarettes – Balkan Sobranies.

"Filthy habit," he said.

I took my time lighting up. The cigarette was very strong. It made me light-headed.

"How have they been treating you here? Well, I trust?"

I studied his narrow face. He had a slight nervous tic. His cheeks were pock-marked

"So, when am I getting out?" I said.

"Within a couple of days, I should think."

I was surprised. I looked away.

"Look, Endicott. One of the reasons I am here, unofficially, is to apologise. We do know what you have been through, and we are grateful, you know. Extremely grateful."

"Really?"

"Oh yes. We do know that you have served your country. I have been looking through your notes. You were at Loos, weren't you? I was in France too, you know."

"In what regiment?"

"The City of London. I was shot up at Mons. Before the war, I was training to be a detective. It was my uncle who got me into this line of work."

"I see."

I was not sure that I wanted to know his life story. I saw

that he was looking at my cigarette, enviously. He smiled and tapped his chest. There was a look of ineffable sadness in his eyes.

"I would love a gasper, Endicott. Can't. Only got one lung, you see. The Boche took the other one. Please ... do enjoy your smoke. I know what these places are like. Now, do you mind if ..."

He pulled a notebook from his pocket.

"Of course not."

"I find it helps, when I get back to the office. Don't have much of a memory, unfortunately."

He licked his business end of his pencil.

"Now then. You are Austin James Endicott. You were born in the borough of Finsbury in 1898. You live at ..."

"I know all this ..."

"Mr Endicott." His face twitched. "I am merely establishing some preliminary details. It is normal procedure."

I felt guilty. It was difficult to be angry with him.

"I understand," I said. "But first, may I ask you some questions?"

"Be my guest."

"The Minerva League?" I said.

"Yes?"

"What do you know about it?"

He took a breath. After a moment, he spoke.

"Endicott, I can understand why you have asked me this. And I shall give you an answer. However, before we proceed, could we just settle one thing?"

I nodded.

"I must ask you never to divulge, to anyone, a word of what I am about to tell you. In other words, this conversation never took place. Do you understand?"

"Of course."

"To give you your answer. Yes, we have known about the

Minerva League since 1913. We have extensive files on its members. Many of them are high-profile individuals. Fortunately for us, they are not very discreet."

"Did you know that they were planning to overthrow the British Government?"

He cocked his head to one side.

"Did you also know that they have worked with the German army to produce a bomb made from uranium and that ..."

"Mr Endicott, these are serious allegations."

"They are more than allegations. Such a weapon has been made. I know that. It was discovered at Tower Bridge."

He looked pained.

"Who told you this?"

"A detective told me, yesterday. This is a rather serious matter, would you not agree?'

He sighed.

"Listen, if it were true then, yes. The matter that you refer to will certainly be carefully looked into. I am not saying that we do not believe you, merely that ..."

"You didn't believe me before."

"What do you mean?"

"You know very well. In October 1914, I was arrested and thrown into prison."

"That is, of course, regrettable."

"Your colleague, Gribley, as good as told me that I would hang."

"Ah, Gribley ..."

"What about him?"

"Mr Endicott." He glanced away. "This too must never, ever, leave this room. I can now tell you that Gribley was not, in fact, what he seemed. He was ..."

"A traitor!"

My face became flushed. The truth had hit me like a

thunderclap. Gribley had not wanted me to be tried in court, because he could not risk me giving evidence. That was why he had packed me off to the trenches. He was working for the other side!

"Where is he now?"

His face looked pained.

"He is in Parkhurst Prison, in solitary confinement. Believe me, he will never see daylight. In all probability, he will kill himself. That is what we are counting on. You see, like many members of the Minerva League, Gribley has certain unusual ... predilections, shall we say. We know about them. And we have made sure that other people do too, including his wife. This is strictly between you and me, by the way." He glanced down.

"You are telling me that he is a ..."

Stokes looked embarrassed.

"Look Endicott. He has shamed us all, let us just leave it at that. It is most unfortunate that he was the first person to read your telegram from Constantinople and that he became your case officer. Gribley is a wrong 'un. At least we have discovered the problem and acted upon it. In all honesty, what else could we do?"

"What about the others?"

"What others?"

"The other members of the Minerva League."

I began to list them – the Prince of Wales, the Duke of Westminster, Brigadier Hinton, Sir James Folie, the Marquess of Abergavenny ...

"What are you saying?"

"Shouldn't you arrest all of them, immediately?"

I could see that he was itching for a cigarette. He satisfied his urge vicariously, by giving me another one.

"Mr Endicott, we live in a democracy. Certain people may have opinions that you and I find repugnant. That does not give His Majesty's Government licence to imprison all of them, now does it?"

"What if they are guilty of treason?"

He lit my cigarette.

"As far as we are aware, the Minerva League is primarily a social organisation. It is associated with certain peculiar costumes and rituals, that is true – so are the Freemasons and the Guild of Fishmongers – but that does not mean to say ..."

"Oh, come on!"

I wanted to be angry with him. But I could not. I wish that I had challenged him now. Perhaps if I had, things would have turned out very differently. Captain Stokes, like many Britons in positions of authority, was a thoroughly decent individual but naive. He sniffed the thin blue smoke with longing.

"Oh, I have some good news for you."

"What is that?"

"It concerns Major Neville and Guy Temple. They have spoken with the Chief Constable or, rather, he has spoken to them and, well ... they are not pressing charges!"

He grinned.

"But Temple tried to kill me. The man is a maniac!"

"Endicott, you took a firearm into his house, and your companion, Miss Bulstrode, discharged it. I have been told that Temple will have a limp for the rest of his life."

"Good!"

I mumbled something else, extremely uncharitable, under my breath. Fortunately, Stokes did not hear it.

"I beg your pardon?"

"Nothing."

"I have some more pleasant news. We are fully aware, you know, that you have suffered inconvenience, loss of income and considerable distress since 1914, when you were arrested."

"Wrongly arrested," I chipped in.

"Yes, quite. And that is why His Majesty's Government is willing to offer you, a sum of money, a one-off gratuity, in the form of, shall we say ... compensation."

He did not give me time to speak.

"This is all unofficial and does not, in any way, imply any liability on the part of the Government or ..."

"How much will it be?" I said.

He looked me in the eye.

"A lot, Endicott. More than enough to get you back on your feet, I should have thought. There is one more thing."

"Yes?"

"There is a condition attached to your receiving the money."

"And what is that?"

"You are not to communicate, in written or spoken form, anything that you know about the Minerva League to any other person. You see, it might interfere with certain lines of inquiry that we are following. You must also surrender to us all evidence that you have obtained about the league."

"What, everything?"

"I am afraid so."

"What if I don't agree to your conditions?"

"We would have to kill you."

I stammered something.

"Only joking!"

His eyes were watery from the cigarette smoke. I noticed that he was short of breath. He offered me his hand. I shook it. Perhaps I should not have done. But the options available to me seemed limited. I could not, in the end, help myself liking the fellow. He was only trying to do his duty. Our business was concluded. We chatted about the weather and prison food. We discovered, by accident, that we shared a love of Middlesex County Cricket Club. Stokes had played a couple of trials for them. He was a useful opening batsman, he told me. At least he had been, before the war.

HM Prison, Lewes
13th of January, 1916

My dear Harry,

Well, here is a turn up for the book. I am back in jail! I am getting rather used to this. I am writing these words in a small room with a high barred window, rather like a monk's cell. It is hard to tell the time of day. The meagre light which is managing to struggle through the window seems to have given up the ghost. The good news is that I shall be out of here very soon – probably tomorrow. You see, I have committed no crime. I am allowed to read and write as I like and to wear civilian clothes. Apparently, I am on the same rations as the prison governer.

After that night in Belgravia, when you disappeared into the storm, I was arrested and threatened with execution. But I was allowed to join the army, in return for my freedom. Later, I became a pilot in a reconnaissance squadron. My job was to fly a pig of an aircraft, called an RE 7. Well, one day I "borrowed" one of them and hopped over the channel, to Kent. I had no intention of being killed before the Minerva League business was concluded. In London I met, by an incredible stroke of luck, your fiancée, Katie Kidd. She was in appearing in a play. She is very talented, by the way.

Katie and I did some sleuthing. I discovered in an extraordinary way (which I will tell you about later) that the Minerva League was still very much in business. I learned, through a haze of opium, that the league has a place down in Sussex – a manor house, with a barn, in which they conduct their disgusting rituals. Katie and I went down there in my motor. We ran into the league on the night of a full moon, close to a village called Rodmell.

I think you can imagine what I saw. It is lucky that Katie did not witness it! It was the full performance – bare-breasted women cavorting around, men with shields, a goat ... Afterwards, Katie and I followed some league members down to the village – a high-brow couple and a whisky-sodden major. They let us into their cottage. When he was in his cups, the major let slip that the league had a new target in view – the Tower of London. It was going to be blown up the following night.

That night, I was discovered rummaging through some papers in the sitting room and there was a shoot out. Katie acquitted herself excellently. She is a brave as a lion and, with a bit more practice, she will be an excellent shot. She managed to blow a man's foot off with my revolver. Unfortunately, I was winged in the thigh. We then locked our hosts in a shed. However, the following morning, a gang of policemen broke in through the front door. The police grabbed us and took us down to Brighton, where we were locked up. They let Katie go but I was taken to Lewes prison – a grim stone building that looks like a medieval castle. A detective interviewed me the following day. He told me that I was to be released. You see, he had spoken to his colleagues at Scotland Yard, who had made investigations after I had telephoned them from Rodmell.

The Metropolitan Police, it would seem, had sent a constable over to the Tower of London, following my tip-off, and he had stumbled across something odd. A large black barge had been moored on the river by Tower Bridge for several days. Nobody seemed to know what it was doing there. When the policeman investigated the barge, he was challenged by a man with a Mauser pistol. He managed to get away and summon help from the Scots Guards at their nearby barracks.

A gunfight took place! It lasted for several hours. Apparently, it was the largest gun battle in London since the siege of Sidney Street in 1911. Of course, you won't see anything about it in the papers. One guardsmen and all of the men on the barge were killed. In the hold of the vessel, the police, the detective told me, found a large quantity of dark grey rocks and half a ton of dynamite. The detective described it as an "unusual" bomb. I think we know what that means, Harry. There was a detonator, attached to an alarm clock. Only a few hours later, the device would have gone off, converting much of east London into a crater.

The best of it is this. I am no longer in trouble, even for deserting. Apparently, conversations have taken place in the highest places and certain strings have been pulled. Unfortunately, we won't be heroes, because all of this is top secret. As I said, I shall be let out of here in no time. I hope that Katie will give be able to give you this letter, which I intend to smuggle out of prison, under the noses of the rather inattentive guards.

One day, I hope to walk down the aisle with you, as your best man, and to make an amusing speech at your wedding reception. With any luck, Ileana will be there too. I miss her terribly and hope to be reunited with her, as soon as the war is over. Katie talks about you constantly, by the way. You have picked a good 'un there, Harry. She is hearty, courageous and a real fighter.

I do not know if they have let you out of the hospital in Lemnos. Perhaps you are on your way back to England. I have been knocked about a bit too. But it is nothing serious. You know I love flying, Harry. Well, I am determined to get myself into a fighter squadron in France. When this grim business is finished, I hope that we shall be able to swap stories, over a drink or two. I am praying that the Minerva League's activities have been curtailed. But, somehow, deep in my bones, I have a feeling that they have not.

By the way, you still owe me five bob from that time in my club! Give my regards to your ma – I hope that she is well – and keep your spirits up. I hope to see you very soon.

Your good friend

Austin.

By some miracle, the sun was shining. But it was pale and tentative, with no warmth in it. As I walked through the prison gate, I felt mixed emotions. Happiness was certainly present, and excitement that I would soon see Katie. However, above all, I was uncomfortable. They had given me a new pair of trousers in prison. They were hot and scratchy. The prison doctor, who had reeked of stale spirits, had mauled my thigh as it were a leg of mutton and bandaged it as tightly as was humanly possible. My kit-bag felt disturbingly light. It had been emptied of its contents. There was one item of evidence that I had refused to hand over to Special Branch – the Blood Stone. There had been a bit of a tussle about it. I had argued that it was not evidence, merely a memento. Also, it was my personal property. Eventually, they had given in.

Captain Stokes was waiting for me outside. He had kindly offered to give me a lift up to London. He wore a belted raincoat over his pinstriped suit and a black hat. He walked briskly, his leather soles clicking on the road.

"There's the old girl."

Ahead of us was a motor car. I recognised the marque from its unusual radiator. It was a Prince Henry Vauxhall. The near-side of the car was battered and scratched.

"Had a bit of prang a few days ago."

Stokes placed his finger on the door.

"Some lunatic forced me off the road. Ended up in the bloody ditch. Tell you what, though," his face lit up. "Whoever it was could shoot the eyes off a gnat. Best piece of shooting I've ever seen. Wish we had a chap like that in the branch."

I muttered something, feeling myself blushing.

"Look," he said, beaming. "I know it was you, old chap. My colleague, Wilson, broke his arm by the way. The stupid thing is, we had absolutely no intention of arresting you. We merely wanted to tell you that we had found about Gribley and that you were in the clear. Ridiculous, isn't it?" He laughed.

"I suppose it is," I said. "No hard feelings?"

"Of course not."

He extended a hand for me to shake. I had no hesitation in doing so. I liked Stokes.

"What is your favourite bowling style, Endicott?" he asked me.

I considered for a moment.

"Full toss, I should think."

"Not a googly then?"

I shook my head.

"Not really."

He reached into the car. He removed some items from the glove compartment – goggles and leather helmets.

"Don't be bashful. Get in. Do you know what the best thing about this job is? Well, one of the best things."

"No, what's that?"

He grinned like a child.

"You can drive as fast as you like!"

Stokes was not a good driver. The problem was, he thought that he was. And he was reckless. People who have been intimate with death often are. Twice, we nearly came off the road when he misjudged a corner. Once, we almost collided with a horse-driven wagon. Stokes waved his fist at the hapless drayman. He tried to talk to me above the noise of the wind. Unfortunately, it was hard to hear what he was saying. Within a couple of hours, we were in London. I had asked him to drop me off at Piccadilly Circus. There was a neat symmetry in this. It had been where the latest phase of my adventure had begun.

Stokes reached across the seat. He pressed a bulging white envelope into my hand.

"I must give you this, Endicott. It's unofficial, if you see what I mean."

He winked. I fingered the envelope.

"You'll find a thousand pounds in there, in brand new five pound notes in there. Counted them myself. I hope that you enjoy the rest of your leave."

"My leave?"

"Oh, I should have told you. You will be expected back with your squadron by Valentine's day, the 14th of February. I have spoken to your commanding officer on the telephone. He was terribly good about everything. He is prepared to forget about your little ... misdemeanour."

"I see."

"Toodle pip then."

Stokes gave a wave. To a chorus of hooters and curses, he slid into the traffic. He had caused chaos in the two minutes that he had stopped. As I watched the car disappear, my mood dipped. I felt that the sense of purpose that had motivated my life for the past two years was vanishing with the vehicle. Also, Piccadilly Circus, with its ceaseless noise and movement, is probably the loneliest place in London. As far as the world was concerned, I was merely a rather shabby and anonymous tourist. However, I knew someone who lived nearby. Katie. She would cheer me up with coffee and rolls. And she would amuse me with her account of her night in the cells. I felt very close to Katie now. The Rodmell experience had cemented our friendship. I knew that we would be talking about it for years.

Chapter Twenty-one

Boisdinghem
15th of March, 1916

Darling Ileana,

I am back in France and I am writing this letter in the mess hut. This is my favourite time of day – before dawn is when my mind is most active. It is when my thoughts of you are strongest. Of course, I think constantly of the time when we shall be together. Is it foolish of me to imagine that you still wish to live in England? Of course, I hope that you will but, whatever happens, I want to be with you. I still have the pressed violet that you left in my room in Dumbrava de Sus. I carry it in my wallet as a token of you. I wish I had something else – a photograph or a lock of your hair. It is the vision in my mind of your sweet, smiling face that keeps me going, especially on the days when we walked by the river and talked of the future. I now think that there will be one, my elf! I cannot give the precise details, but I was recently in London. I was reunited with my house and my old car – you know, the Singer. I ran into some desperate characters. Because of what happened, I think that they have been put out of action – at least, I hope they have.

It was strange to come back to the squadron at Boisdinghem. Jagger, my fitter, was delighted to see me again. He had made a small garden behind the hangar and planted it with winter pansies and wallflowers. The weather here is drab and grim, but it cheers my spirits to see something neat and orderly and a splash of colour. It reminds me of English gardens and of country railway stations. It also suggests that there will be a summer, although God knows what it will bring. The Germans have been piling into the French to the south of *here. You would not believe the volume of the artillery barrage – you would not want to be beneath it – and the brightness of the sky at night as it flashes with star shells. Soon, it will be our turn. Most people think that something really hot will go off in the next few months. Perhaps it will end this murderous stalemate. I hope that I shall be making a more significant contribution than taking photographs in these rattling old buses that I am forced to fly. I have applied to transfer to a more active squadron. Do not worry and please keep safe for me. Know, my elf, that I am praying for the time when we shall be together.*

Fondest love

Austin

In January 1917, I gained my wish and joined a new fighting unit. Number one was one of the first three squadrons of the Royal Flying Corps. In 1912, it had acquired the balloons, airships and kites of the Royal Engineers. Its motto was *In omnibus princeps*, "first in all things". Its badge, strangely enough, was not dissimilar to that of the Minerva League – it was a winged number one, surmounted by a crown. In the month that I joined, the squadron took delivery of a brand new aircraft – the Nieuport 17. The Nieuport, a French machine, was small and light, with a rotary engine. British versions of the aircraft carried a forward-facing Lewis gun on an ingenious sliding rail mounting. This had been designed by a chap from No. 11 Squadron.

The machine was a true "fighter", a single-seater specifically designed for combat. It climbed like a witch and had excellent visibility. The fact that it was rather slow was more than made up for by its manoeuvrability. French pilots had enjoyed wonderful successes with the Nieuport 17 and had become national heroes. We took to it like ducks to water. Until the SE5 and the Sopwith Camel appeared in numbers, it was unquestionably the most effective allied scout.

I had tasted blood now. In April, which was a catastrophic month for the RFC, I made my first kill – an Albatros. I shot down four more in the next month and a Fokker E III. My seventh victim was a Roland C II. Escorting a bombing mission, I encountered three enemy aircraft. I managed to break them up and bring one of them down in flames. My Nieuport was virtually destroyed and my forehead was grazed by a bullet but I limped back to the aerodrome. This was what won me my DSO.

I was now a veteran with more than a year's flying experience under my belt. I could have become an instructor in one of the new flying schools, teaching terrified cadets how to get off the ground, but I did not wish to. It was not because I was brave. Almost half of the RFC's pilots were killed in training during the war. I simply could not face adding to the death toll. In June, I was promoted to captain and made a patrol leader. I had not sought the post. I preferred flying on my own, if the truth is known, but I had little choice.

That July, the tide for the RFC was turning. Earlier in the year, we had been losing fifty aircraft a week. Now, with new tactics, better-trained pilots and superior machines, we could take on the German squadrons and even mix it up with them. Sometimes, we would run into Manfred von Richtofen's "flying circus". This was a group of hand-picked pilots, who roamed up and down the lines at will, picking off whatever targets took their fancy. They were easily distinguishable, because their aircraft were painted in bright colours. Their leader, Richtofen, was a former cavalry officer. He was a flamboyant character; his Albatros D III was bright scarlet. He had been trained by the great Oswald Boelke, the systematizer of German aerial fighting techniques. We had bombed his aerodrome at Douai in April. Seventeen bombers had blown up fuel and ammunition stores. Richtofen was playing cards with his comrades in a shelter. He walked away unscathed.

One August afternoon, I took up a Nieuport on my own for an afternoon sortie. The air was hot and thick. It had been a day of thunder-storms and a golden sun, slanting through dense clouds. Far below, around Ypres, the tortured ground was being fought over yet again – it was Haig's idea to capture the Ypres salient, the high ground that overlooked the town, and to break through to the Belgian coast. His attack had been ruined by torrential rains. Most of Flanders, whose drainage ditches had been destroyed by shells, was a boggy morass. The British attack had been stopped in its tracks. In the past two weeks, tens of thousands of men had had been pulverised by shells and machine guns and sucked into the slime.

Tracking the Menine Road, on the allied side of the front line, I saw some enemy activity. A thousand feet below, seven or eight German triplanes were harassing three RE8s. These slow-moving British two-seaters were used mainly for bombing and reconaissance work. They were long outmoded. The triplanes were painted in rainbow hues. My heart sank. It was the flying circus! It had just been equipped with the brand new Fokker DR1, a copy of the Sopwith Tripe Hound.

First, I touched the Blood Stone, which I kept in an inner pocket of my flying jacket. I always did this before going into combat; it was my only superstition. I pulled the joystick to the right and kicked the rudder bar hard with my right foot. The Nieuport's nose rose up and then dipped. I went into a steep dive. I watched as my airspeed climbed – 120, 130, 150. The wind screamed through the cockpit and a force like a huge hand pushed me back into my seat. The lower wings of Nieuports had been know to tear off in situations like these – it was somewhat worrying.

One of the Fokkers was yellow, a second was painted in a harlequin livery, a third was an improbable blue. It was a shade of aquamarine that almost hurt the eyes. There was no sign of Richtofen's red scout. He must be elsewhere. Thank the Lord. Even so, things did not look too hopeful. The Fokkers wheeled around the RE8s like gaudy birds of prey, firing their twin machine guns. The situation was hopeless. Soon, a wisp of grey smoke trailed from one of the British machines. The observer jerked like a straw dummy as tracer bullets slammed into his body. He slumped over his Lewis gun, as a red stain spread from his head across the fabric-covered fuselage. The RE8 was doomed. I pulled out of my dive and flew at the tripes. For a second, the bright blue Fokker, embellished with crisp German crosses, was in my sights. The pilot turned his head to look at me. If it had not been for his helmet and goggles, I would have been able to see his expression. I squeezed my trigger. There was a brief burst and then ... nothing. The confounded gun had jammed. I could have rammed him – such things were not unknown in dog fights. But I had no wish to sacrifice my life, just to get bar for my DSO.

At the last possible moment I wrenched back my stick. My undercarriage almost brushed the Fokker's upper wing. I now made a difficult manoeuvre, an Immelman turn. It was a combination of a half loop and a roll. Looking back, I saw an uplifting sight – a flight of Sopwith Camels had appeared from nowhere! The Camels dived among the Fokkers and scattered them. The scene now became a confusion of red and blue circles and black crosses as the planes rolled and dived. It was now every man for himself. I had challenged the honour of the blue Fokker. Sure enough, it broke off to pursue me. It was faster than my Nieuport. I must not let it get behind me. We must have circled each other like mad men more than twenty times. All the time, the Fokker was gaining on me. I tried my

Lewis gun again. It was still jammed.

Two or three miles away, a bank of black clouds was heaped up over the Ypres salient. Every so often, a yellow flash would flick out from its base, like a snake's tongue. Rain must have been lashing down on the poor devils in the trenches below. Even in the position I was in, I would not have changed places with them. Perhaps I could reach the clouds? It was not much of a strategy, at best a delaying tactic. Pulling out of the turn, I began to zigzag. The German pilot would have been smiling. Many of his victims would have resorted to the same trick.

There was a sound like tearing paper. Bullets tore into my upper wing, leaving neat black holes. Horrified, I saw dents appear in the metal cowling around my engine. Suddenly, a twist of smoke appeared. Something important had been damaged. My adversary must have been changing a drum, for there was a hiatus. Soon, he would finish me off. I did not want to be a "fryer". That's why I always carried my loaded Webley with me. I was reaching into my jacket, just in case, as my propeller touched the vast storm cloud that was darkening Ypres.

The cloud was as damp and cold as a cellar with the light turned off. A choking mist, compounded of petrol fumes and half-burnt oil engulfed the cockpit. The fuel-starved engine was sick all right. It began to misfire. My best bet would be to get to the ground to make a forced landing. If the Fokker followed me, I would be a dead duck. It would be firing directly down on my cockpit. The air was black and bitter, as if a fresh delivery had just been poured down a coal chute. I was almost blind. Realising why, I wiped my oil-filmed goggles with the back of my glove.

Squinting, I now saw a strange red blur ahead of me. Was it blood? No, the blur was moving. And it had wings! They were beating economically, propelling the shape forwards. I had seen something like this before, in Transylvania. You may find this hard to believe, but it was a dragon! The huge creature was about fifty yards ahead of me. It craned its long supple neck, to check if I was still behind. I could tell, somehow, from this gesture, that the dragon was on my side – that it wished me no ill. I felt a warmth spreading from my chest. Had I been shot? I reached into my flying jacket to investigate. The Blood Stone, I discovered, was hot to the touch. It seemed to be pulsing, in time with the dragon's slow wing beats.

I stayed on a level course, following the dragon. The engine was spluttering. It was only just holding out. The cloud thinned. To my surprise, we emerged, suddenly, into the open air. The cloud had disorientated me. I saw that I was directly over the Ypres salient, heading north over the German lines. I was going the wrong way! The dragon kept up a steady progress. Suddenly, something alerted it and it turned back. The Fokker, I realised, had also come out of the clouds. It had scented blood and was hurtling towards me. Within seconds, the German would open up his guns and deliver the *coup de grace*.

The dragon made a tight turn, of which Immelman would have been proud. For a moment, the great beast seemed to hover in the air, like a heron landing on a lake. It emitted a gigantic roar and a stream of fire issued from its mouth, like a viscous orange liquid. A blast of heat passed directly above me. It seared the top of my head. The fire was precisely targeted. I watched, as it engulfed the azure Fokker. The machine dissolved. Its fabric and wood components were consumed within seconds. In a flaming ball, it dropped from the sky. I would hazard a guess that only the engine, some wires and rivets and a half-melted human body reached the ground.

Looking forwards, I made two discoveries. First, the dragon had vanished into thin air and, second, flames were leaping from my engine. The propeller was now feathering. It was a fine calculation whether I could glide to the ground before I had burnt to a cinder. There was nothing in the way of grass below – only remnants of forests, in seas of shattered stumps, miles of mud and water and villages which looked as though they had been thumped by a giant fist.

With flames streaming around me, I scanned the ground for a likely spot. Close to the Belgian village of Zuidhoek, I found it – a patch of corrugated cow pasture, next to a narrow brown stream. The Nieuport almost shook itself to pieces as I wrestled it to a stop and jumped, if that is the right word, down from the cockpit. My cheeks were blistered, my eyeballs felt as though they had been sprayed with sand. Through a haze, I saw three figures in grey uniforms running towards me. A true hero, no doubt, would have fought to the last bullet but I felt, at that moment, that I had done everything that my King and country could expect of me.

Without hesitation, I flung my revolver to the ground and thrust my hands in the air. Luckily for me, the German soldiers were gallant enough to accept my surrender. The four of us watched, silently, as my aeroplane crackled merrily, lending some brightness to a dull evening, like children around a bonfire. Soon, there was virtually nothing left of it. Prodding me with their rifles, the soldiers led me across the field. I did not ask them if they had seen a blue Fokker downed by a flame-breathing red dragon. Mouthing a silent prayer, I touched the Blood Stone, marvelling that I still alive. I was fortunate indeed. I spent the remainder of the war as a prisoner, initially in Belgium and then at a horrible place in Bavaria.

Chapter Twenty-two

Harry came into the room. His brow was moist and he looked
uncomfortable in his dark suit. However, it was relatively cool
in the library; this leather-scented world provided relief from
the fearsome heat that was pounding London's streets. I had
been surprised when he had asked to see me at short notice.
Harry had phoned Croydon aerodrome, where I was working
as a pilot for Imperial Airways, from his office in Fleet Street.
It was August 1934. He was now senior foreign correspondent
on the *Daily Express*. It was not *The Times*, as he had wished.
But the *Express*, as Harry often told me, had the largest
circulation of any newspaper on the planet – more than two
million. Its magnificent black marble office, recently opened,
was the envy of the world. I motored up from the airport
immediately after his call. It was a sweltering Thursday
afternoon, I recall – the sun was blistering the tarmac.

"Captain Endicott. How are you?"

A playful smile bared his white teeth.

"I am well, thank you, Captain Hawkins," I said.

It was a curious fact that both of us had attained the same
rank – Harry in the army and me in the Royal Flying Corps –
and an even more curious fact that we had both survived the
war. Harry walked with a stick. He claimed to have enough
shrapnel in his chest to fill a sandbag. My body had its share
of wounds and my legs were stiff but they were just about
strong enough to manage the controls of a Handley Page
airliner.

We shook hands.

"Just like the old days."

"That's right," I agreed.

Harry looked around the room, silently noting its details.
Familiar books were in the same places on the shelves where
they had always been. The Travellers' Club had been deserted

for a few years after the war. Now a new generation of adventurers had appeared – chaps who made light of the Alps and who were venturing into the Himalayas, with oxygen tanks. Harry and I, both in our 40s, had become the old guard.

"Please, take a seat."

Harry winced as he settled into an easy chair. It grieved me to see him in pain. But he would never have admitted it.

"Would you like a drink?"

He nodded.

"Is Harrison still here?"

"Dead, I'm afraid." The old waiter must have been at least seventy when he had popped his clogs. Now, there were new members of staff – distracted young men who did not seem to know who we were.

"I'll ring the bell."

We had the library to ourselves – a dusty sanctuary with thick damask curtains.

"What's it all about then, Harry?"

I sat facing him. Strangely, we were in exactly the same positions as twenty years before, when I had first told him about the Minerva League and he had suggested my trip to Transylvania.

"I'm worried, Austin." His face looked pained. "I'll come straight to the point. I met this fellow, last month. He was an Oriental. He came to the office and asked from me specifically. I took him to a chop house off Ludgate Circus. He was extremely nervous. Wouldn't go to a pub."

"And?"

My friend frowned.

"I have seen him a few times since then, always in different places. He has told me something that has disturbed me profoundly."

It took a lot to worry Harry. What on earth could it be? He leaned forwards.

"My contact, let's call him Fu Manchu, is the manservant of a certain English nobleman. The young chap has a penchant for cocaine, apparently, and fast young ladies. He lives, at least when he is not on the grouse moors or in the south of France, in a large house in Eaton Terrace."

He leaned forwards.

"The thing is, a group of people regularly gets together at his house, for dinner parties. It's an intriguing set – actresses, blue bloods, rising politicians. Do you know the playwright Noel Coward?"

"Of course," I said.

"He knocks around with them. Sometimes, they meet at his place at Goldenhurst, down in Kent. Then there is Poppy Baring, the Maharini of Cooch Beha and, last but not least, Prince George, the Duke of Kent. It would seem that Coward and the Duke are lovers."

Had Harry gone mad? He was simply regurgitating London tittle-tattle. He sensed my unease.

"Listen, Austin, this meant little to me either, until my contact, Fu Manchu, happened to mention the name of another member of the group – Sir James Folie. Do you remember him?"

How could I forget him? He had been a leading light in the Minerva League. It had been in Folie's mansion flat that I had been arrested in 1914. I had spent the following year in hell.

"Another frequent visitor to Eaton Terrace is Lord Londonderry – you know, the Secretary of State for Air. "

"So ..." I must confess, I was regretting, somewhat, my hot, dusty journey from Croydon.

"Austin, don't you see where all of this is leading? Ah, good ..."

The waiter had finally arrived. There was a hiatus, while he fiddled with glasses.

"Very well," said Harry, after the waiter had gone, "let me

put it all together for you. Tell me this. What is the most important field of warfare, in the modern world?"

My mind went blank.

"I'll help you. It is the air. He who has control of the air, and, specifically, of aerial bombardment, can win any war. The airforce today is what the navy once was."

"Now ..." He could see that he had me under his spell. "Which politician controls Britain's Royal Airforce?'

"Lord Londonderry," I said. "He is responsible for the numbers of aircraft produced, and so on."

"Good."

"Now. Do you know anything about Lord Londonderry's politics?"

"No."

"Let me fill you in. Lord Londonderry is a dilettante – an aristocrat with a vast personal fortune and lots of time on his hands. He is not, shall we say, the brightest button. He only got his job because he has a pushy wife who knows Ramsay MacDonald. But he does have distinctive political views. He is an admirer of Adolf Hitler. I know what is crossing your mind," Harry paused. "What does this have to do with us? But please, think for a minute."

"I'm trying."

"Good. Here's how it works. Londonderry, through his social contact with Sir James Folie, learns how to make a uranium bomb. We know that he runs the airforce and that thinks that Hitler is a good chap. What do you think that this means?"

I made no reply.

"Shall I spell it out it for you? Londonderry, through intermediaries, passes the secret of the uranium bomb to Hitler. He tells Hitler that all the materials he needs to make a very nice bomb are in an old quarry, in Transylvania. They just need to be dug out. Londonderry gives Hitler assurances that

Britain will sit on its hands while Germany builds up its airforce and won't do very much to expand the RAF. In fact, why doesn't Hitler have the RAF? It will be delivered to him, lock, stock and barrel, once Britain and Germany become allies."

I thought for a moment.

"Do you think that he has done this, or that he will do this?"

"I have no idea. It's my guess, from what I have learned, that overtures have already been made to Hitler. Plenty of British people like fascism, you know."

It was true. The *Daily Mail* had run many flattering stories about Sir Oswald Mosley, leader of the British Union of Fascists. Working with Hitler, or ignoring him, was favoured by both left-wing pacifists and aristocratic Conservatives. Winston Churchill was one of the few politician with the guts to say that Hitler should be stopped. He had made a speech recently, I recalled, about the overwhelming importance of air power.

Harry had always had the ability, since school, to take a few threads of fact and to weave them into a garish tapestry. I could see, from his benign expression, that he was utterly convinced of his theory. It did not sit happily with me. For you see, for the first time in my life, I was a contented man. I should explain that I had rescued Ileana from Romania after the war (that was an advenure in itself, let me tell you), brought her back to England and married her. We were living in a charming cottage in Ashtead, in Surrey, and had a beautiful daughter, called Eleanor.

Ileana baked cakes and made jam. She had become a stalwart of country life and a keen member of the Women's Institute. I loved my job and it was reasonably well-paid. As a commercial pilot, I flew a luxury airliner to Paris, Brussels and Basle. Sometimes, I flew over to Imperial's base in Egypt,

Cairo, and had a tour of duty on the eastern routes. Now, I supposed, Harry would want me to give it all up, and shoot off on some crackpot mission, which would almost certainly end in mutilation and death. My mutilation and death. Why the hell didn't he do it?

"Why don't you tell your editor about this?" I said.

He looked down at his now half-empty glass.

"Would do, old chap. But I'm pretty sure that he is working for MI 5. If I told him, I might just as well send a telegram to the air ministry."

We heard laughter in the corridor. The club's evening shift was beginning.

"What do you want me to do about it?" I said, tetchily. "Fly to Romania, I suppose, parachute out of the plane and ..."

"Austin, Austin ..." Harry looked shocked. Sometimes, he had the softest, kindest eyes.

"I am not asking you to do anything. Who else could I tell about this?"

"You could try your readers."

"Yes. But I expect that I should soon fall victim to a mysterious accident if I did that."

I sighed. So, it had started again. Hawkins and Endicott versus the world's greatest evil. Why did it always have to be us? Another member came into the club – a young, supercilious fellow in a tennis blazer with carefully trimmed blond hair. He ignored us. There would be no second drink. I would give Harry a lift back to Sydenham, I decided, in my Invicta.

"Listen," I said. "This fellow who you met in the chop house, who told you about Lord Londonderry, what did he look like?"

"As I told you, Oriental. Yellowish skin. Long black hair."

"What was his name?"

Harry looked around. It was not a state secret, but he spoke softly.

"Culadar. His name was Culadar."

"I see." I could feel my heart thumping.

"Harry," I said, "are you sure that is what he was called?"

"Yes, why?"

"About how old was he, would you say?"

"Hard to tell. He was a youngish chap, late twenties perhaps? Is there anything wrong, Austin?"

"Good grief."

"What's the matter?"

My friend looked at me with concern.

"I think that I met the same fellow," I said, "in Whitechapel, twenty years ago. And he was not a baby."

"Are you sure?"

"Yes."

"But that is impossible."

Harry looked as if he had eaten something that did not agree with him.

"One could hardly forget a name as unusual as that," I said. "A few years ago, I jotted the named down on pad and, do you know, I discovered something interesting."

"What was that?"

"That name, Culadar, is an exact anagram of the well-known fictional character, Dracula."

"So?"

"Dracula, in Romanian, means 'son of the dragon'."

Harry looked at me blankly.

"Don't you see? It connects with something that my friend, Radu, told me, when I was in Transylvania."

"Please enlighten me."

I took a breath.

"Well, that part of the world is extremely superstitious. Radu explained to me that, in ancient times, a pagan religion was practised in Dumbrava de Sus. Its adherents worshipped dragons. They even made sacrifices to them."

"What are you getting at?"

"I believe that it is possible that this ancient Romanian religion – this cult of the dragon – still exists. Those who follow it have access to supernatural powers. They are the sons of the dragon."

"And we have met one of them?" Harry gave me a funny look.

"Yes."

"A man who did not grow a day older in twenty years? Do you really expect me to swallow this rubbish, Austin?"

My friend, for all of his imaginative flights of fancy, was a deeply practical creature. It was partly because of his trade. He viewed all occult phenomena – whether spiritualism, ectoplasm or fairies at the bottom of the garden – with equal disdain.

"You may believe whatever you like," I said. "All I know is that I have seen dragons, twice. The first time was inside the Devil's Mountain. The second time, a dragon materialised from thin air and saved me from certain death, when I was being chased by a Fokker over Ypres. I also know that, on two occasions, a man named Culadar has given us clues that have allowed us to thwart the Minerva League. That is an extraordinary coincidence, don't you think?"

Harry did not reply.

"Perhaps," I continued, "the Minerva League and the sons of the dragon are pitted against each other. Perhaps they always have been. Perhaps both have access to vast, elemental forces."

"Vast elemental forces." Harry sighed.

"I have been reading about this," I said, warming to my theme. "You see, dragons are always female in mythology. And their blood is always held to have magical properties, like witches' blood. It is a cosmic battle, Harry. On the one hand, we have the feminine principle of the earth, which is guarded by dragons. Christianity calls it evil, but it is nothing of the kind. On the other hand, we have a masculine form of human power. It is attempting to steal that which belongs to the dragons, in the service of a truly horrible cause. You see, Harry ..."

"For heaven's sake!" my friend guffawed. "Admittedly, you may have experienced some weird hallucination in a cave. And you may well believe, in good faith, that a dragon saved your life in a dogfight. But quite honestly ..."

He looked away. I noticed, then, how shabby the club was. The leather chairs were scuffed and scratched, the carpet was almost as grimy as the pavement outside.

"Look, Harry, I began ..." I was about to expand upon a Manichaeist theme – all human life, I would have reasoned, was governed by forces of light and dark, or, in Christian terms, good and evil. Both needed each other. They were interdependent. However, it was perfectly possible for light to call upon the forces of darkness and vice versa. And sometimes, the equilibrium that held the world in balance was lost.

"What?" he said.

"Nothing," I said. The devil, at that moment, seemed a remote fancy. "Would you like a lift back to Sydenham, in my motor?"

Harry gripped the arms of his chair in mock terror. He used to joke that I handled a car like an escaped lunatic – a role that I played up to.

"Must I?"

"I'm afraid so."

I patted his good leg.

"Very well. If you insist."

The young man in the blazer gave Harry and I a cursory glance as we left. He barely saw us. To him, we were two hopeless old fogeys, one with grey hair, the other with a stick.

Harry's words played on my mind a lot. But I did not do anything about them. There was a lot of badness in the world at the moment, I reasoned. And I was getting a bit too old for heroics. A couple of weeks later, on a Saturday, I was sitting in the staff room at Croydon Airport. Inevitably, because so many of Imperial's staff had served with the armed forces, it was called the mess. It was a lovely morning. The sun and the wind were just right. I was to pilot a chartered flight to Cologne today. Ashburton, my first officer, had just come in. He was nervous because it was his first flight as second in command. Conditions were perfect, I had reassured him. His job would be a piece of cake. In those days, before radar, it was only possible to fly in daylight. Navigation was largely a matter of following roads and railway lines.

From the passengers' point of view, the Handley Page HP 42 was the last word in comfort and elegance. Its cabin was almost as long and wide as a Pullman car; it was fully carpeted and there was a stand-up bar. There was an excellent view, because the cabin was slung beneath the upper wing. Once, airline pilots had been stuck out in the open but now we had an enclosed cockpit. The HP 42, an enormous, four-engined biplane, was very slow – it cruised at little more than a hundred miles per hour. But it was extremely stable and you could land it on a sixpence. Passengers loved it. They could eat meals, drink cocktails and play bridge as they drifted over the shifting panorama of the British Empire. They were well-served by Imperial Airways. For its routes now extended from Croydon as far as South Africa, India and Singapore.

Ashburton looked uncomfortable in his brand new uniform. I had ribbed him that he must have been up all night, ironing his shirt and starching his cuffs. He did not smile. Woolley came in then. He was my boss. Like me, he had been an RFC pilot in the war. In 1919, he had had the foresight to go into commercial aviation. His small company had been absorbed by Imperial Airways in 1924. He was a cheerful soul. He was wearing his customary clothes – an open-necked shirt, Oxford bags and golfing socks. As usual, he was on his way to the links. He kept his clubs in the office, he said, so that his wife did not know where he was. Of course his wife, Ethel, always knew where he was, to the nearest inch.

"We have royalty today, Endicott," he said.

"I'm sorry?"

"His Royal Highness, the Duke of Kent is in the passenger hall. Just bumped into him. He has a large group in tow. They're a bit rowdy, I'm afraid."

I was surprised. Today's flight had been chartered in the unobtrusive name of George von Wettin.

"The duke tells me that he fancies himself as pilot," said Woolley. "How about giving him a crack at the controls?"

He winked. Aristocrats were not the most popular pupils. Usually, they combined arrogance with a reckless disregard for their personal limitations.

"Of course. He can bring us down for re-fuelling in Paris," I joked. "Bertie can show him the ropes, can't you?" Bertie was our nickname for Ashburton. The young man looked worried.

"Don't worry," I said to my first officer. "You never know, the Duke of Kent might take a shine to you."

Woolley laughed. He stood in the doorway of his office.

"Oh, Endicott," he said. "There is something that you should know. Some of the duke's party are carrying flags – swastikas."

"Swastikas!" I was horrified.

"It seems that they are going on from Cologne to a political meeting, in Nuremberg."

"What kind of meeting?"

"Apparently, it is the annual rally of the Nazi party."

"With Hitler?"

"No, with Charlie Chaplin." Ashburton did not laugh. Woolley continued. "I imagine that if Her Hitler is not there, hopping around like a flea, they will be extremely disappointed. The duke told me that he knows Hitler rather well. In fact, they are having dinner together, tonight. Perhaps you would care to join them?"

I did not know what to say. Woolley remained in the doorway.

"Look, Endicott," he said, "I know you are not very happy about this. Neither am I. The fact is, their money is just as good as any one else's. Just do your job, get them to Cologne and come back. Hold your nose if you have to."

We stared at each other. He, like me, hated the Nazis far more than the Germans that we had fought in the war.

"Is that understood?"

"Yes, sir," I said.

"Good man."

His door clicked shut. Woolley liked a drink at this time of day. Come to think of it, he liked a drink at any time of day.

We had started the second port engine. Now all four of the Bristol Jupiters were firing up nicely. Soon, I would signal for Ashburton to taxi us to the end of the runway. There was only one problem with the HP 42. Visibility from the cockpit was extremely poor when one was on the ground. There was a loud knock on the thin plywood door that separated the flying crew from the forward cabin.

"Sir, sir!"

Paolo's head pocked through. He was our steward. He was an Italian, with a dark complexion and a large Roman nose. It was Paolo's job to keep thirty-eight passengers fed and watered – to give them receptacles be sick into and to cater for their curious and often unreasonable demands. This lot was straining his patience to the limit. They were weighed down by picnic hampers, bulging suitcases and shooting sticks. It had taken upwards of an hour to get all of their luggage on board – and they were not grateful or appreciative. Quite the opposite, in fact. The aircraft had been rocking gently, in time with their boisterous antics. From behind, I had heard the sound of smashing glass. I had dispatched Ashburton to calm them down – pretend that you are Hitler, I had suggested. He had returned white-faced. If anything, the noise had got worse after that.

"Sir, I think that ..."

Suddenly, a figure barged past Paolo, pushing him rudely out of the way. It was a short, thin man with sandy hair. He had the same pinched yet handsome face as his father, King George V, and the same penetrating eyes. The man's breath was sour with wine. Another, stronger smell lingered around him - it was perfume. He spoke with a slight stammer.

"I am ready to take the c ... c ... controls!"

"I beg you pardon?"

"The controls. I am a pilot, you know. I am taking lessons."

The Duke of Kent squeezed past the wireless operator. It was impossible to stand upright in the cockpit. He stooped in front of me, glaring. His black suit dropped loosely from his narrow shoulders. I noticed something. It made my heart quicken. In one of his lapels was a tiny enamel badge. It was a five-pointed star, with wings – the symbol of the Minerva League! Suddenly, everything that Harry had told me slotted neatly into place.

"I wish to take the controls," the duke slurred. "You will show me respect and do as I say."

I stared straight at him. Ashburton hunched down into his seat, trying to make himself invisible.

"I shall do no such thing," I said.

"I beg your pardon?"

"I am the captain of this aircraft. As such, I have sole

responsibility for the safety of its passengers and crew."

His eyes narrowed.

"Do you know who I am?"

"I believe that you are a minor member of the royal family," I said, my hackles rising. "But, as I have explained, I am in charge. If you do not leave my cockpit, I shall have you escorted from the aircraft."

"You and that bloody little Jew, I suppose."

He was referring to the steward.

"I do not think that I heard you."

He placed a hand on his hip.

"That bloody Jew boy."

"Sir," I said. "We are in England, not Germany, and you will leave my cockpit. Now."

He took a breath, squaring himself up, like a bantam.

"How d ... d ... dare you!"

Suddenly, he lunged at me. Alcohol had loosened his inhibitions but it had also removed his sense of balance. The lunge became a sprawl. Poor Ashburton took the brunt of it; the duke threw up as he fell, showering my first officer with vomit. He threw out a hand to protect himself as he toppled forwards. This became firmly wedged between Ashburton's thighs.

"Oh, my God."

It was the strongest expression I had ever heard my first officer use. Ashburton did not have a sense of the ridiculous; the situation – an unfamiliar hand thrust into his groin – was merely mortifying to him. The duke began to curse, his mouth flecked with sick. Fortunately for me, his horizontal position rendered his threats ineffectual. He muttered that he was a personal friend of Lord Londonderry. He would see to it that my pilot's licence was revoked. He would also complain about the appalling inadequacies of Imperial Airways, and so on.

Paolo came sheepishly through the door. A couple of men

in dinner suits pulled the duke out of the cockpit and brushed him down. Quiet words were spoken. The passengers were exhilarated by the prospect of the Nuremberg rally; to abandon the trip seemed inconceivable. I took off, as quickly as I could, hoping that alcohol would blur the duke's memory of what had happened.

On the way back, I realised that Harry's forebodings had been right. The Minerva League was up to its old tricks. And I now had conclusive evidence that one of its senior members was in direct communication with Hitler, the German Chancellor. I needed to talk to my friend, urgently. As luck would have it, Harry was coming to Ashtead for lunch the following Sunday, with his wife, Katie Kidd.

Chapter Twenty-three

Katie Kidd, had been extremely successful in the past few years. After the war, she had made a name for herself in musical theatre. In the 1920s, she had broken into silent films, usually romantic comedies. She had married Harry, at the first opportunity, in 1919 at St Bride's Church in Fleet Street, and I had honoured my promise by being his best man. Harry's press and army friends attended in equal numbers and the wedding was a joyous affair. I acquitted myself fairly well in my speech, because Harry was an easy person to burlesque – he had a relaxed attitude to life, combined with a propensity to blunder into astonishing situations.

I told the story of the night in 1914 when he had introduced me to the art of house-breaking, in Belgravia, and then abandoned me to my fate. How brave was he really, I speculated? After all, I had a DSO whereas Harry had merely been awarded the Military Cross. By a neat symmetry, Harry was my best man, when I married Ileana in 1921 – the year that Transylvania was liberated from Hungary. He was also godfather to my daughter, Eleanor, who was born a year later. Not that I had ever associated my best friend with habits of piety or godliness.

Katie stood in the conservatory of my cottage in Ashtead. It was a Sunday morning in September, a week after my flight to Germany. She and Harry had motored down from London from their new house in Sydenham. Harry was in the kitchen. I could hear him talking animatedly to Ileana, who was preparing a meal. Katie was wearing a brown taffeta dress with a plunging v neckline, set off by a string of pearls. I would not say that success had made her conceited – her feet were still planted firmly on the ground – rather that she was radiant with success; it seemed to glow from her face. She had been talking to my daughter, Eleanor, about the film that she was making for Warner Brothers, in Teddington. Errol Flyn was the star. The subject had then moved on to animals. Eleanor was twelve. She had her mother's smile and her curly hair, but hers was darker. We used to joke that she was our little gypsy.

"I would love to see him. Would you show him to me?" Katie said.

"Daddy, could I show Katie my pony? Could I, please?"

Eleanor looked at me, imploringly. How could I refuse?

"Of course," I said. "But don't be too long. Lunch is almost ready, darling."

"Thanks, daddy." She had large brown eyes. We had no idea where they had come from.

"Come along!" She took Katie's hand.

I watched them walk down the garden. At its far end, a door led to through a wall covered with climbing roses to a field, which I rented from a local farmer. That was where Eleanor's pony, Teddy, was kept. Katie looked back at me, before she ducked and went through. She was smiling. For a moment, I thought I saw something odd in her eyes. I could not put my finger on it, but I had a presentiment that something was wrong. An instinct. Unfortunately, I did not do anything about it. I went into the kitchen.

As I entered, a delicious aroma of roasting meat and herbs greeted my nostrils. Ileana was cooking our favourite Sunday lunch – pork and onions. She turned from the oven and smiled. Her elfin face with its sparkling blue eyes filled me with an intense joy. I could see that she was trying to concentrate – she had been talking about this meal and assembling the ingredients for days. Harry would have been distracting her, in the nicest way.

"Harry," I said, "what on earth are you two talking about? You seem to be getting rather worked up."

He turned to the doorway.

"I was asking Ily what she knows about the Iron Guard."

"The what?"

"It is a Romanian branch of fascism. It is led by a fellow called ..."

"For God's sake, Harry," I said, "Ileana is not in the least bit interested in that kind of thing. She hates politics. She finds the subject utterly boring."

"No, no, it is not true."

Ileana protested but I knew that I must rescue her from Harry. He could not help asking people lots of questions. It was his job. However, Ileana probably knew less about Romania's geography and politics than our village postman.

"Come with me," I said. "Firstly, you have no right to be in the kitchen and, secondly, I have something to tell you."

"If you insist. You are sure you do not mind?" He smiled at Ileana.

"Of course she doesn't. Come on."

We went back into the conservatory. I had built it myself, just after we had moved into the cottage, in 1922. It was a lovely place to take meals on summer evenings, while enjoying the scent of honeysuckle and stocks from the garden.

"Well then," said Harry, "what is it?"

"It's about the Duke of Kent," I said.

"Yes."

"You have heard of the annual Nazi party rally, in Nuremberg?"

"Of course."

"Well, last weekend I had to pilot a chartered flight to Cologne. There was a party from London going on to the rally. It was led by the duke. I met him – he had appalling manners, by the way. The man is a Nazi."

"I know," Harry said. "Everybody does. So is his brother, the Prince of Wales."

"Well, it came as rather a shock to me," I said, "especially

when he started dishing out anti-Semitic abuse to my crew.
But there is something else."

"What is that?"

"He was wearing a badge in his lapel."

"Yes ..."

"It bore the symbol of the Minerva League."

Harry breathed out slowly.

"That is bad news," he said. "But, I must say, it is not
exactly a surprise."

"The duke has been holding meetings with Adolf Hitler," I
continued. "That means that he may have passed on the
league's secrets to him, about uranium. The situation is just as
bad as you told me, Harry."

"It certainly puts a new complexion on things." My friend
reached into his pocket for a cigarette. He was going into a
reflective mode.

"What are we going to do?"

Harry shrugged.

"I don't know. But I'll tell you what, I'm damned hungry.
That food smells delicious. What did you say it was called?"

I told Harry the Romanian name.

"Where is Katie?"

"She went into the field, to see Eleanor's pony."

"Did she tell you about her new contract?"

"No."

"She has just signed with MGM. She will be going to over
Hollywood in February."

"Really, Harry? That is wonderful ..."

There was a loud bang, like a car misfiring. It came from
the direction of the garden. We both knew what it was, from
our war experience – a small arm.

"Oh Lord ..."

I have rarely moved so quickly. I bolted down the garden
path, like a startled deer. Harry was close behind me. The door

to the field was open. We did not stop until we reached the stable. Something gave me pause. I stood outside the brick building. Breaths were rasping from my chest. I could hear something awful – a child crying. The sound tore at my innards.

"Austin!" Harry hissed into my ear. "Don't go inside."

It was too late. I saw a man, in the shadows. He was holding a gun and there was a smirk on his face. On the other side of the stable, Eleanor and Katie were pressed back against the wall. Teddy was lying down, his legs twitching. Red foam was bubbling from his snout. A pool of blood spread out from his muzzle.

"He killed my pony, daddy!"

Eleanor looked at me, imploringly.

"Shut up!"

The man stepped forwards. In his right hand was a long-barreled pistol.

"Get against the wall!"

I saw his face. It was pale, with a Rasputin beard. I had seen the face before. But where? It was the sneer on his pink lips that gave it away. It was Guy Temple, the man who Katie had shot in the foot in Rodmell, twenty years before.

"Daddy, is Teddy ..."

"Shut up!" He licked his lips. "Now, I am going to kill all of you. The barrel of his gun moved fractionally – towards me. My time is up, I thought. My last memory would have been the impression of leering triumph on his face. It was the same look of evil that I had recognised in Rodmell. There was only thing I could do. Take a lunge at him.

There was a loud bang and a flash. Temple's forehead caved in. For a second, he remained upright. His eyes were staring. They were mad, bright eyes. I shall always remember that. He reached up, tentatively, as if to touch the wound. It was fairly clean. Most of his blood and brains had showered from the back of his head, leaving a dark red stain on the wall. He looked surprised. His body swayed and he toppled forwards, like a tree. By a strange chance, Temple's arm flopped against Teddy's chestnut belly. His hand was extraordinarily white. We discovered later that his fingernails had been polished.

"Good grief, Harry."

My friend's face was expressionless. There was no triumph there. He had turned very pale. Calmly, he replaced his gun in his jacket pocket. Eleanor began to sob, touching her pony. Katie comforted her. We covered Temple's body with Harry's overcoat. Then we went back into the house.

Winston Churchill's house, Chartwell Manor, was a large, red-brick affair – imposing, in its own way, but surprisingly plain. It stood on a lip of land overlooking the flat green plain of the Weald. Churchill's view of Kent was spectacular. The house had extensive grounds with numerous outbuildings. Here, the former Chancellor and First Lord of the Admiralty would amuse himself by building walls and daubing oil paints on canvas, when he was not writing books or speeches in his study. He was the kind of man who must always be doing something.

We drove there in my S-type Invicta, passing, rather quickly, through Reigate and Oxted. The same niggling worries were troubling both of us. What if Mr Churchill thought that we were both mad? Perhaps it would have been better to dispose of Temple's body and cover our tracks. But then, the killing had been self-defence and there were three witnesses. Surely, no judge or jury would convict Harry. Unless they were members of the Minerva League. In which case, he would hang.

"All right, Harry?"

I had slowed down to a crawl, having entered the village of

Westerham. I was scanning the side of the road for the turning to Chartwell. It was a grey, misty morning. The weather was far too dull for the momentous thoughts that were passing through our heads.

"Not bad," my friend said, doubtfully. "You know what?" he continued. "That swine must have stayed in the stable all night. He was just waiting for his chance to have a crack at us. Did you notice – there were matches in his pocket but no cigarettes or pipe. I'm pretty sure that he would have killed all of us and then set fire to your cottage."

"Somebody must have told him that you were coming to lunch," I said.

"I know." Harry turned to face me. "That's the worrying thing. People must be watching us, Austin, and passing on intelligence to the Minerva League. Do you think it's Special Branch?"

"I don't know," I said. "I gained the impression from that chap I met in Lewes prison, Stokes, that the secret services are now on our side. But still ..."

Harry said he would make some discreet inquiries. He told me that he knew someone who knew the head of Special Branch, Basil Thomson, socially. Of course it would have to be done very carefully.

Going to see Churchill and telling him everything that we knew had been Harry's idea. I had been sceptical. But Harry had assured me that Churchill was as solid as a rock. He knew everybody in the British establishment – he was related to most of them – and he had an implacable hatred of fascism. Trust me, he had said. Hadn't I trusted him on that madcap jaunt across Romania and on the night we had gone thieving in Belgravia? I had pointed out that taking our story to Churchill was high-risk. It could end with us both being arrested. Harry said that I should have faith in his instincts. As usual, he had won me round. At least being with him was never boring.

"It's Eleanor I feel sorry for," said my friend. "It' such a shame that Temple killed her pony."

"Isn't it," I said. "What a bloody swine. Of course, I shall get her another one. But she loved Teddy."

We fell silent. Chartwell is approached by one of those pretty, leaf-fringed lanes that are scattered through Kent – a green, light-dappled tunnel. Churchill must have passed this way in his chauffeured car, on the days that he was sitting in the House. It was the kind of lane that makes you feel happy that you are alive and that your country is free of tyranny.

The road ahead was pleasingly straight. I changed into top gear. The S-type was low to the ground and had a throaty six-cylinder engine. Harry crossed himself, as he was thrust back into his seat. Was he joking? He always said that driving with me was terrifying. There was an exhilarating roar as I pushed the Invicta to maximum revs. The beech trees to either side became a green blur. We seemed to leave the dead pony, the Minerva League and the horrors of Flanders and the Dardanelles far behind us. Harry gripped the sides of his seat. The whiter I could make his face, the happier I would be.

From the depths of Churchill's house, came a deep, muffled clang. It was Harry who had pulled on the bell. It seemed to take an eternity for a butler to reach the door. The servant treated us with disdain, as if we were selling clothes pegs. It took every ounce of Harry's persuasive powers, which were considerable, to get us inside. But he managed it. Eventually, after a lot of huffing and puffing, we were ushered into an antechamber and told to wait. We did – feeling extremely nervous – for three-quarters of an hour.

Churchill was wearing a silk dressing gown. I noticed that it was splattered with oil paint. He was smoking an enormous cigar. At first, there was a ferocious scowl on his face, but his mood softened as he listed to our tale. He invited us into his drawing room, where we continued our narrative. Speaking in turn, Harry and I told Churchill everything we knew about the the Minerva League, right back to 1914, and the uranium mine in Transylvania.

He listened attentively. He appeared to know a lot about the destructive properties of uranium. At the conclusion of our story, he told us that an Italian, called Fermi, was continuing the theoretical work of Sir Ernest Rutherford in Manchester at the beginning of the century to break down atoms to release their energy. We were on friendly terms now. Churchill invited us to take lunch with him. We declined, insisting that it far was too much of an imposition. However, we would be happy to join him in a whisky and soda.

What about the dead body in my stable? Churchill said that it was a mere formality. He would telephone his friend, the Chief Constable of Surrey, and that the matter would be dealt with, unobtrusively. To my astonishment, it was. Churchill assured us that he would act upon the information that we had given him. He was particularly shocked that his cousin, Lord Londonderry, was "in cahoots" as he put it with Hitler. With reference to the perfume-loving Duke of Kent, he assured us that not all members of the royal family were bad apples.

Churchill showed considerable interest in Harry's experiences in Gallipoli. He said that the disastrous Gallipoli landing would almost certainly have been successful but for the fact the navy had stopped its bombardment of the Turkish coast too soon, and the dithering of certain military commanders. He was deeply sorry that things had turned out so badly. Before we left, he insisted on showing us the painting that he had been working on when we had disturbed him. It was a still-life, depicting some fruit. I had feared that Harry and I would be confronted by an embarrassing daub. In fact, to our great relief, the painting was not bad.

Everything that Winston Churchill told Harry and me at Chartwell in September 1934 actually came to pass. Guy Temple's body was duly collected by policemen that evening and slid into a canvas bag. The men had no warrant numbers and did not smile. An inquest into Temple's death, in Guilford, found that he had been killed in a "shooting accident". Lord Londonderry – a bumbling amateur in world of professionals – lost his job the following year, when Stanley Baldwin, the nation's favourite pig-keeper, became Prime Minister.

On the 22nd of May, 1940, the government invoked Defence Regulation 18B. This gave the Home Secretary extremely widely drawn powers over those who endangered the safety of the realm. Over the following week, although we did not know about it until later, virtually every known member of the Minerva League was arrested and imprisoned. Most of them had it pretty soft. But at least they spent the war behind bars. When an atom bomb was unlrashed, on the 6th of August, 1945, it was not by the Germans, but by the allies.

History records that the Duke of Kent was killed in a mysterious flying accident near Braemar in Scotland on the 25th of August, 1942. He was at the controls of a Sunderland flying boat with 15 men on board. Accounts are contradictory but most agree that his aircraft exploded. All but one of the people on board were killed. A granite memorial at a lonely spot on the moors records the event. Official accounts say that the duke was on "active service" heading for Iceland, in order to make a "tour of inspection". However, this version of events is pretty unconvincing.

It sems highly probable, if distasteful, that the duke was attempting to broker a peace deal with Hitler. There is even a theory that Hitler's deputy, Rudolf Hess, who was held prisoner at Loch More, nearby, was on board the aircraft. For this theory to be correct, there must have been two Rudolf Hesses and the one who was later held in Spandau Prison by the allies was an imposter. This may be going a little too far. But it is hard to escape the conclusion that the bisexual duke, a loose cannon, forfeited his life through his indiscretions and that he was killed by the Special Operations Executive, on the orders of Winston Churchill. If that is the case, it will never be corroborated by official documents.

Churchill was forced to abandon Chartwell for the duration of the Second World War – it was far too conspicuous a target for German bombers. From its upper storeys, in the summer of 1940, he would have had a grand-stand view of the Battle of Britain. He must have been immensely gratified, after his fears in the 1930s, that the RAF was equal to the task and that the Luftwaffe was found wanting.

One bakingly hot August afternoon, I witnessed a lively skirmish between British fighters and Messcherschmidts in a cloudless sky over Croydon aerodrome. I watched as a flight of Hawker Hurricanes from my own No. 1 Squadron put up a lively show against the Germans. My whole body was tingling. How I wished that I were up there too! The Hurricane, with its Rolls Royce Merlin engine and its tubular steel frame, could fly at more than 300 mph on the level. That was a machine! I could not wait to go up in one. But that would have to wait until after the war.

Further copies of Dragon Rising can be obtained from from Honor Oak Publishing, 7 Buckley Close, Forest Hill, London SE23 3EQ